Sisters
of the
Seventh
Planet

Teri Hoskins

BALBOA.
PRESS

A DIVISION OF HAY HOUSE

ISBN: 978-1-4525-6240-7 (sc)
ISBN: 978-1-4525-6241-4 (hc)
ISBN: 978-1-4525-6239-1 (e)

Library of Congress Control Number: 2012920706

Balboa Press books may be ordered through booksellers or by contacting:

Balboa Press
A Division of Hay House
1663 Liberty Drive
Bloomington, IN 47403
www.balboapress.com
1-(877) 407-4847

Because of the dynamic nature of the Internet, any web addresses or links contained in this book may have changed since publication and may no longer be valid. The views expressed in this work are solely those of the author and do not necessarily reflect the views of the publisher, and the publisher hereby disclaims any responsibility for them.

The author of this book does not dispense medical advice or prescribe the use of any technique as a form of treatment for physical, emotional, or medical problems without the advice of a physician, either directly or indirectly. The intent of the author is only to offer information of a general nature to help you in your quest for emotional and spiritual well-being. In the event you use any of the information in this book for yourself, which is your constitutional right, the author and the publisher assume no responsibility for your actions.

Any people depicted in stock imagery provided by Thinkstock are models, and such images are being used for illustrative purposes only. Certain stock imagery © Thinkstock.

Printed in the United States of America

Balboa Press rev. date: 11/20/2012

This book is dedicated to my soul sister
SANDI MCCARTHY
May we have many more adventures together!

PREFACE

When I was 24 years old, I was walking through my living room when I clearly heard, "Someday you'll write a book." I stopped in my tracks and looked up toward the ceiling wondering where the voice had come from! My next thought was, "No, I won't. What would I write about?" Then I heard the voice again, "Yes, you will."

"No, I'm just a stay at home mom; I have nothing to say or to write about." I thought.

That was two years before I discovered Ramtha and his teachings. Ramtha and JZ Knight have been my teachers since 1987. As a student of Ramtha's School of Enlightenment (RSE), I've studied quantum physics, neuroscience and ancient wisdom. I've learned how to access extraordinary abilities that exist within my own mind. I've been taught that everyone can tap into the mind of God and experience the remarkable.

After attending RSE for several years, the book started writing itself in my head. As the book made itself known to me, I wrote it down on scraps of paper, napkins, in notebooks, whatever was handy in the moment. I talked a lot about writing the book, but never actually sat down to do it. I knew

I was supposed to, but I didn't know how, so I procrastinated for several decades.

But the book would never leave me alone for long. I could go months without it speaking to me, but it was always lurking in the background. Shortly after my father's death, the pressure to right the book wouldn't leave me. It no longer lurked in the shadows, now it openly haunted me all day long.

I was driving to work one morning arguing with myself on whether I should write the book or not. My strongest argument was that I didn't know how to write a book, I knew nothing of the industry; I had no idea how to even get started. I had never taken a writing class, at least not since high school. Then suddenly all these years later, I heard the same voice again, "You don't have to do anything, the answers will come to you."

"Oh right!" I thought to myself, like that will ever happen!

Later on that same day, a new client came in. While making small talk, I causally asked, "So, do you work outside the home?"

"Well, actually, I'm an author," she responded.

I shared my story with her, and of course, she was more than happy to tell me how to get started and what steps to take. I had finally run out of excuses. So I sat down on November 1, 2010 and started writing it. Since then, the doors have opened easily and two years later, I now have a completed book!

The book is the first of a trilogy. It is a work of fiction, yet, I've woven personal experiences, the latest science, ancient wisdom and Ramtha's teachings to create a fantasy. It is my hope that the book brings joy and wisdom to your mind and soul.

Enjoy!
Teri

Acknowledgements

I have been fortunate to have many people believe in me and encourage me to write this book. It took a lot of prompting on their part, but after more than twenty years of talking about it and dreaming about it, I finally acquiesced and wrote it. It is impossible to name all those that have played a role in bringing this book to its fruition but a few stand out in my mind.

I owe great thanks to those that read the manuscript in its beginning stages and offered their advice, Sandi McCarthy, Joy Merritt, Karen Phillips, Helen Pressley, Sheryl Simpson and Dr. Jon Taylor.

Deep appreciation is given to my mother, Joyce Arne and my sister, Penny Rasmussen for their contribution. Without my editor, Lois Winsen, you would have been forced to read all my grammar and writing errors! Many thanks to my friend Jenny Bankston for believing in me and for providing the character's name, "Shriya", to Chris Kaitlyn for always listening and supporting me, and to Joann Clarkson, a writer herself, who has always encouraged me.

This book would have never been written if I hadn't been a student in Ramtha's School of Enlightenment (RSE). So my heartfelt thanks to JZ Knight and Ramtha for teaching me that God lives within all of us and providing the disciplines so that I've been able to experience the miraculous myself.

Prologue

I feel the flames rising up around my ankles; I close my eyes and pray as I shake with fear, "My beloved God, raise the vibration in my body so I do not feel this pain. Allow my spirit to soar quickly towards you. Relieve me from the burden of this physical body."

My sister and I are tied to a stake, our hands bound behind our back; our shoulders touching each other. Her hand grabs mine, gently squeezes it, and I feel her love flow through my body. It eases my fear enough to open my eyes. Through the smoky haze I see someone struggling through the crowd. My daughter! I hear her scream, "They're killing my mama! They're killing my mama!"

I close my eyes again and ask my beloved God to spare her from this scene. My heart aches as I realize how this will affect her, the emotional pain and heartache she will suffer because her mother is accused of healing the sick. The Priest will punish her no matter what she does or doesn't do; he will hate her just because she is my daughter. The daughter of a witch is a stigma she will never live down.

I open my eyes again and look over at the Priest as his face breaks into an evil smile. His biggest fear is that the townspeople will recognize the divine power which lives within each of them. My sister and I have always been an enormous threat to his control over the people.

As I look out at the crowd gathered to watch us burn, I see many of the women and children we have healed over the years. That they stand by and say nothing causes me deep emotional pain that hurts more than the burning flames at my feet. I have dedicated my life to the healing arts, and saved many of their lives. Yet they will allow their fear of the priest to overrule what they know to be an atrocity.

Suddenly I hear my daughter scream as I see her push frantically through the crowd, "They are killing my mama! They are killing my mama! Will you not defend them? They have saved many of your lives; will you not save theirs? Will you not stand up to the Priest? He has no power over you, only the power you have given him. Please help them, please! They are killing my mama!"

CHAPTER ONE

APRIL 3, 1540

I COULD HEAR THE TOWNSPEOPLE WHISPER behind our backs as my sister, Gwenneth, and I walked through town. Most of them would never acknowledge us, but their eyes were on us. I suspected their dislike for us had something to do with our mother's death. I'm not sure how our mother died. Gwenneth won't talk about it. One day I pushed the question, and quickly learned I'd made a mistake. I had forgotten how stubborn she can be. Once she makes up her mind about something, she won't budge. She looked at me with scorn. "It's in the past and we don't live in the past. It doesn't make any difference; she's gone, and that's what we have to deal with." Her lips clamped into a thin, straight line. End of subject. So I didn't bring it up anymore.

I reached over and held her hand to help me feel better. The townspeople made me uncomfortable. Gwenneth sensed my uneasiness and said, "Shriya, do not be afraid. We are proud women, proud of our ancestry, and proud of what we do. If it weren't for us, many of these women and children would be dead now, so know they are grateful, even if they don't have the courage to show it in public. Remember, if any of the men found out their women had come to us for healing, they would be stoned, burned, or at least tortured, and they can't risk that. So be happy you don't have to live in the daily fear they do."

Her words, meant to comfort, didn't make me feel better. We are natural healers, it is in our genetic line. But because it was against the law, we had to be careful. If the Priest ever found out, we would be imprisoned or possibly killed. He didn't take the act of healing the sick lightly. Apparently it was an evil thing to save one of God's creations. This state of mind was a mystery to me. I could never understand the concepts of right and wrong held by those who made the law.

As we walked through the market's front door, a woman rushed past us almost knocking me over. I recognized her as the woman we healed last week of a broken arm. No doubt she saw us coming and was in a hurry to avoid having to speak to us, or even being seen with us. The fact she wouldn't even look at me reminded me how lonely I was, and how different from the townspeople. I did not worship the Priest.

Janna, the market owner's wife, greeted us with a warm smile, "Gwenneth! Shriya! What brings you to town?"

"We have eggs to trade today," Gwenneth answered. I knew we had actually come to town to find out how a child is doing. The child was brought to us with a sickness the Priest could not identify. The little boy's skin was yellow and he had been throwing up for several days. Gwenneth and I immediately recognized his problem as an imbalance with his liver. We did everything to heal his frail body. Now it's simply a matter of time to see if he will recover. It will be up to his soul to decide if he is going to stay in this life or not.

Janna brought women and children to us for healing when the Priest failed in his attempts. We lived in tumultuous times when fear ran rampant, a time when the Priest used his power to entrap the town's people into his way of thinking. He threatened them by saying they would be burned in a place he termed "The Pit". According to the Priest, "The Pit" was an underworld of horror, where they would be confined for eternity by an evil gatekeeper. Because of this, the townspeople were called "worshippers" since they blindly worshipped the Priest.

Janna looked around to make sure we were alone, then whispered, "It took the boy several days, but he seems to be doing fine. His color is back to normal, and he has not vomited since we left your house."

Gwenneth sighed in relief, "Good, I have been concerned about him. When I tried to look into the future, I could not see what happened. I worried we had not been successful."

"I think he will be fine, and his mother is well pleased with what you have done." Janna said.

"Will she thank us in public?" I wanted to know.

Janna looked at me with sympathy in her eyes. "I'm sorry Shriya, she lives in fear of the Priest. You know the Priest creates all the laws for the land. He insists everyone obey them without question. The Priest tells her what to believe. She cannot believe in you, your sister or your healing abilities."

"How can that be?" I said in disgust. "How is it she will accept the healing of her son, but not believe in it? That doesn't make sense."

Gwenneth looked at me. "Shriya, she cannot outwardly believe. Even if she believes it in her heart, or knows it to be true from experience, she will never admit it. Her life depends upon denying it."

"What is a life created out of a lie?" I asked. "If she cannot speak her truth, what point is there in having a life filled with fear?" Gwenneth gave me a stern look as if to say, "Be quiet." I ignored her.

"Janna," I said, "we are healers, it is natural to us. Our ancestors have been healing for hundreds of generations. Because it is now against the law, doesn't mean the people shouldn't stand up to the Priest. My sister and I are as much at risk as the townspeople. If the Priest ever finds out what we do, we will be imprisoned or perhaps even put to death. As I see it, our risk is equally great."

I was tired of arguing the same point over and over. I had this same discussion with my sister many times and learned that the fear of survival is bred into humans instinctively, so I would never be able to win using logic. I turned around to walk outside.

"Don't go too far, Shriya," Gwenneth said as I went out the door. "And stay away from the docks!"

I pretended not to hear her. I walked past the cobbler's shop and waved to the cobbler. He was one of the few men in town who was pleasant to us. His full gray beard hung down to his chest, and sometimes I could see little bits of food stuck in his mustache. One day, when I was quite little, I found myself staring at him. He looked over at me, smiling, while wiping off his mustache. He finally said, "Do I have food in my mustache, little one?"

"No," I replied, "Are you a grandpa?"

"Yes, I am."

"I thought so, because you look really old." I knew by the look on my sister's face I had said something wrong. "Well, he does," I replied in my defense.

He laughed and said to Gwenneth, "It's alright, she is right. I am old!" I looked at Gwenneth triumphantly. But that didn't stop the lecture I got on the way home. I had to hear about how sensitive people can be, and how telling the truth is considered rude. I began to understand it isn't always acceptable to say what you think.

This day I could smell the stench of blood in the air as I walked in the direction of the butcher. Even though I ate meat, I did not enjoy taking the life of another soul. However, as Gwenneth reminded me often, "A carrot screams just as loud when it is plucked from the ground as a bull does when it's slaughtered. Because you cannot hear the carrot scream does not mean it doesn't have a soul, too." So I made it a habit to bless any food before I took its life, whether it was a berry from a vine or a chicken my sister was about to behead. I made sure I thanked it for its sacrifice so my body would be nourished and allow my life to continue.

As I walked through town, I heard laughter coming from the ale house. The men in town could go there and purchase alcohol made from grain. Females weren't allowed to enter. Well, some women were allowed, but apparently none of the other women in town liked the ale house girls. I don't know why. I often wondered if the ale house girls felt left out and as lonely as I did.

As I strode toward the docks, I took a deep breath of the fresh air rolling off the bay, and filled my lungs with its salty tang. I looked at the boats tied along the dock and saw a few big ones, the kind that could go out to sea for a week at a time. They belonged to families who made their livelihood from supplying fish to the town. I saw smaller boats used for pleasure. People took them out to enjoy the luxury of floating on the water for the afternoon. I always wanted to do that.

Gwenneth told me my wish was unreasonable. "You can never go out on a boat," she said. Even so, I loved to stand on the dock and watch them. Gwenneth did not allow me that privilege often. When we came to town, we got what we needed quickly, and left as soon as we could.

The truth is, though I loved to look at the boats, I was actually looking for someone. But I couldn't let Gwenneth know. She didn't want me to talk with any of the young men in town, especially any good looking ones. But there was one boy in particular I looked for every time I stood on this dock. I saw him from a distance last year. He was walking away from me, heading towards the ale house. There was something about the way he moved and carried himself which made my body quiver. Since then I hadn't been able to get him out of my mind.

I was lost in my own thoughts as I looked at the beautiful blue water gently rippling across the bay, when suddenly… there he was, right in front of me.

"Good day, Miss," he said to me.

At first I was so surprised he wasn't ignoring me like the others, I didn't know how to respond. So I just stood there looking into his brown eyes. He had long black hair, high cheek bones, and his skin was a deep golden brown. He was beautiful, and when he smiled at me, I melted. I could almost hear my heart pound against my chest as he spoke. He looked somehow familiar, and my mind raced as I tried to place him. He interrupted my thoughts by asking if I had ever been on a boat before.

"No, I haven't. But someday I would like to."

"Well, maybe you can come out with me sometime." He pointed. "That blue and red boat over there is mine."

"Yours?" I asked in surprise. The boat was about 50 feet long and had a cabin at the back with several windows on the side. The bow was a crimson red, and the cabin a deep blue.

"It is my family's boat. We are fishermen and have been for many generations. It is how we make a living. My brother and I love to fish. We provide fish to all the villages up and down the coastline."

I had heard of the fishermen before. They are tribal and live leagues away out to sea. The Priest does not care for them; he says they are not equal to the townspeople. The tribesmen hunt and fish for their food as all barbarians do. Locally, farming is the only accepted method of producing food. The Priest says it is God's intent. To show his disapproval of the fishermen, the Priest made a law banning the eating of fish on weekends. Because of it, the large fishing boats were not allowed here during those days. It is another law I found ridiculous. But for a long time I had given up trying to make sense of the Priest's laws. I believe he made them up because he had the power and could do it.

The young man before me didn't appear barbaric at all. He had strong muscles that gleamed as the sun shone down on him. I felt stirrings in me I had never experienced before.

"You are a tribesman?" I asked.

"Yes, I am. My name is Parkin."

"My name is Shriya. We raise fruits, vegetables and some livestock on our land.

"We?"

"My sister, Gwenneth, and I."

"Oh." He seemed to sigh in relief.

I could not tell him we were healers, although I wanted to. I felt a strong desire to be honest with him, but I didn't know him. Or did I? He looked so familiar. I felt I'd known him before, even before I saw him from afar for the first time some years before. I was twelve now and I guessed his age as fifteen or sixteen.

I heard Gwenneth calling, "Shriya, there you are. I have been worried and looking for you. Do not sneak off like that again." She saw I was in the company of a young man. Her eyes grew large, and she grabbed my arm and said to Parkin, "Excuse us, we must be going." She turned me around abruptly and quickly walked me away.

"Gwenneth, why are you behaving like this? He is not a worshipper, he is a tribesman." I tried to explain, hoping to banish her concern.

"I know exactly who he is, Shriya."

"Really, you do? He looks so familiar to me, I feel I already know him. Who is he?"

"Someone to stay away from. I don't want you to talk with him again," she snapped.

I was taken aback by her attitude. "How do you know him?" I asked again.

"I know his type. That is enough. I warn you to stay away from him."

The tone of her voice surprised me. She was being extra stern with me, and apparently wasn't going to give me any type of explanation. Sometimes I'd get so exasperated by her stubbornness. But I knew when she took that tone, there was no arguing, so I dropped it. She instructed me to go and sit under a nearby tree, then turned around and headed back towards the docks. I knew this could not be good. I assumed she was going to speak with Parkin and I didn't want to know what she would say.

My brief encounter with Parkin set my emotions in full flood. Infatuation suffused every part of my body as Gwenneth and I walked back home. She could forbid me to speak to him, I thought, but she couldn't stop me from dreaming about him. I had dreamed about him ever since the first day I saw him from afar, wondering what it would be like to be in his arms, and imagining he was my best friend, the one person I could tell anything to.

Yet, my dreams at night were more like nightmares, and always the same. Parkin and I were on a boat together. Suddenly he disappeared overboard. I searched for him. As I ran from one end of the boat to the other. I screamed his name. When I woke from these dreams I was covered in sweat and sobbing, as if I had suffered a substantial loss. Why was my grief so real? It was a mystery. The thought of losing him devastated and confused me.

I walked over to a tree and leaned against its strong trunk. It was a sunny day and the heat sapped my energy. Under the tree's leafy boughs there was relief from the heat. I rested my head against the bark and closed my eyes. I soon saw bright colored lights come towards me, and had the sense of being drawn down a long twisting tunnel. I felt myself become lighter and lighter, my body weightless. I was floating. I slowly opened my eyes and didn't know where I was. I marveled at the intense red and pink stripes on the horizon of the sky above me. I looked down and realized I was in midair! In a panic I looked at the ground, wishing I was standing on it! In that same instant I was back with my feet firmly planted on the ground. I breathed a sigh of relief. I looked out to sea, but it appeared different than it had a few minutes ago when I was standing on the dock looking for Parkin.

Then I saw him, not alone as before, but with a young woman. I trembled as I looked closer to see who he was with. Suddenly I sensed the presence of another "being" beside me. The "being" felt large and loving. It said, "You are looking at a scene from the distant past, as you and Parkin walk along the dock toward your boat. Neither one of you are aware a storm is coming. Parkin was your husband in that past, lost when he fell overboard during a storm."

"What are you saying?" I asked.

"You are being given the opportunity to see yourself in a previous lifetime."

"Why? I don't understand." Oh! The recurring nightmare came rushing back to me. I recalled the anxiety of seeing him go overboard, and shouted, "Parkin, don't go! Don't go!"

"They can't hear you. You are in a different dimension, vibrating much faster than the plane of existence they are on. There are many dimensions and many lifetimes. What you are witnessing now is your past. Do not confuse it with your future." And with those words, the "being" disappeared. But I continued yelling, "Don't go, don't go! There's a storm coming. You'll drown!"

I woke up to hear myself yelling. Sweat streamed down my brow. I sat up, my back stiff from leaning against the tree, and looked around to see if anyone heard me, but I was alone. I wiped my face and stood up on wobbling legs. I wanted to run and find Gwenneth to tell her my dream. But I wondered, was it a dream or had I really been in another dimension? I decided to keep this experience to myself. I was afraid of what she might say, and really afraid of what she might do.

CHAPTER TWO

GWENNETH AND I WALKED BACK to our home in the woods. After the incident in town; neither one of us was very talkative. I looked at her and noticed she had aged. She was only eight years my senior, yet she looked much older than twenty. She had been taking care of me since our mother died. At that time, I must have been about three or four years old. Gwenneth could only have been about twelve, but was forced to grow up quickly, and watched over me like a loving mother. Over the years we had become very close.

As we walked down the long road, I thought I saw a few fairies out of the corner of my eye. I could hear them, but when I turned my head to look, they disappeared. My inner sight wasn't developed enough for me to see them well, but I knew eventually it would improve. For the time I found it frustrating to see the tiny creatures only in my peripheral vision. If I let myself drift into a light trance as I walked by, I could hear their laughter and feel their joyfulness in the air.

We lived next to a beautiful patch of woods where animals, fairies and forest creatures roamed freely. Forest creatures protected their territory from those wishing to harm the land. Fairies and plant spirits, assisted humans by curing ailments of the physical and emotional body.

Our house, built of clay and straw, had been in our family for many years. We are descendants from an ancient civilization which had practiced the art of healing and other paranormal abilities for hundreds, maybe even thousands of years. We observe society and try to help them by using our knowledge and abilities whenever we can. Thanks to my family lineage and education, my mind had developed faster than the mind of an average child of my age.

I was relieved when our home came into sight. I wanted to sit down and relax by the fire, close my eyes and relive the afternoon's experience with Parkin. I was too excited to do any chores, and didn't want to try to do any inner sight exercises. I wanted to daydream about Parkin and think about seeing us together in our past life.

Those thoughts were quickly put to rest when we reached our front door. A wounded doe lay directly to the right of it. The poor creature had been attacked by some predator. Blood gushed down her torn open left leg, exposing her muscles. I immediately placed my hands above the wound while Gwenneth ran to the garden to pick an herb that would relieve the deer's pain

I calmed my mind, eliminated my daydreams of Parkin, and soon accessed a deeper level of consciousness. As I sank deep into the realm inhabited by unconditional love I started to see an indigo color. At first it came in small bursts. Then it appeared like a kaleidoscope; with purple and blue colors mixing in different geometric shapes. I could sense God's universal love beginning to flow from my hands.

I held this state of mind until I could no longer see the deep colors in my mind's eye, then, slowly let my hands fall to my side, opened my eyes and saw my sister smiling at me. I expected her to be at the head of the doe, helping me. Instead, she said, "I am so pleased with you. When I came back with the herb, the animal was already in a deep sleep from your healing hands. You have progressed far with your abilities. You did a great job today. Look at her leg, it is almost completely healed."

I looked at the doe, and noticed the only sign of its previous wound was the lack of hair on her leg. Then I realized the sun was setting.

"How long did it take?" I asked.

"You have been here for almost two hours," Gwenneth replied.

I had truly lost all sense of time, for it felt as if only a few minutes had passed. Thanks to Gwenneth's years of hard work with me, I had finally reached that deep place in my mind…a timeless place where unconditional love flowed without boundaries, a place that brought peace and joy to my entire being.

I got up and made my way to the lake. The light frost on the grass crunched with every step I took. I loved walking there, and could see the tall mountains in the distance as I navigated towards my favorite spot. It was one I had chosen years ago, where I could sit quietly and enjoy the beautiful view.

When I was six years old I created a little altar along this side of the lake, slightly hidden from view because of the thick woods. Once I had finished it to my satisfaction, I looked around for a new adventure. I noticed a small pathway hemmed in by brush, and decided to explore it. It was too narrow for an adult, but I was small enough to wriggle my way through, and eventually came upon a clearing. The sun was just rising over the trees, shining so brightly it made little lights dance and sparkle on top of each wavelet on the crystal clear lake. It was magical. I sat mesmerized as I imagined each dancing light was a fairy. As the lights danced, they grew closer to me. The closer they came, the brighter they got until *Poof!* they disappeared. I sat there, stunned. What happened to the dancing lights? I stepped closer to the lake's edge and looked down into the water but saw nothing except my own reflection. I was an ordinary looking girl. My dark brown hair hung straight down my back. My nose was long and straight, and I hated it. Even at six I knew I was not as pretty as the other girls in town. But I also knew I was different in many ways.

I sat at the water's edge for some time. Eventually the water started to become misty, and on its mirrored surface different shapes began to appear. I blinked, and blinked again. I rubbed my eyes and instead of seeing my reflection, I started to see images of others. I saw the neighbor at our house, talking with my sister. He seemed upset about something. He flung his arms around as he spoke and my sister shook her head as if in sorrow. Then the image broke, and I saw only water.

I ran all the way home to tell Gwenneth about the amazing lights. As I got closer, I saw the neighbor in our yard talking to her. His arms were flying around as he spoke in a loud voice, "Now they want us to pay tax on the food we barter with. Will it ever end?" I stood there bewildered as I watched my sister shake her head in disbelief. Suddenly I realized this was my recent vision come to life. I stood transfixed as another realization took hold. I had discovered an unusual lake; a lake that could show me the future. I knew I had a secret. At the time I was too young to understand it was not the lake; it was the state of mind I had put myself in which allowed me to glimpse into the future.

I was a carefree child, allowed to explore all depths of nature. Excited about my discovery, I decided the lake would now be my favorite spot. I began to collect special rocks I thought were pretty, brought them there and set them in a semicircle. In the center of the semicircle I placed a memorable pink stone, a rose quartz crystal my mother had worn around her neck. A few precious stones had been passed down through the generations. They were respected and revered for the vibration frequency they held. Each rock I brought spoke to me in a different way. I don't mean I could hear them speak. They spoke to me by the way they made me feel.

From that time on, I woke up every morning about an hour before sunrise. I would make my way to my meditation place on the lake so I could be with nature before starting my day. Of course, as I got older, I had to cut myself a path. Once I grew over five feet tall I didn't enjoy crawling under the brush anymore.

Once again I sat cross legged facing the lake, about to practice an ancient breathing technique as the sun was about to birth another day. The sacred breath technique raised my energy level and kept the energy flowing freely throughout my body. As I sat at the lake and looked over at the mountains, I felt grateful for my life. Soon I would celebrate my thirteenth birthday, a significant event. Becoming a woman would open the possibility for me to pursue my dream of being with Parkin. I dreamed about him nightly, and envisioned him holding me tight and kissing me for the first time. I allowed myself to imagine Gwenneth surprising me by inviting Parkin to my birthday celebration.

In exactly one week I was going to turn thirteen. It would be a momentous day for me because our custom on such an occasion was to give a focus wand to a child studying the sacred knowledge. My birthday would mark the beginning of my journey into adulthood. My body was about to start to produce hormones that would flood through me and cause the energy to drop from my brain down into my reproductive organs, a period of life called puberty. A focus wand would give me the help I'd need to keep energy up in my brain, and develop my inner sight. When we are young we can sense, hear and sometimes see fairies and magical forest creatures, but once the energy starts to drop, we lose these abilities.

Our planet floats in a sea of ether we call the energy field, which vibrates at an extremely high rate and is empowered by the mind of God. The mind of God is a universal power that conforms itself to the thoughts we have, and transmutes them into physical reality, allowing us to experience our thoughts first hand.

My sister and I were initiates of the sacred work -- knowledge passed down to us from our ancestors. Although the mind of God is an intangible force, it can be harnessed and managed through the human brain by those trained to do so. Initiates of the sacred work are trained to manipulate and command the energy field, even transmute physical matter by harnessing the ether into a focused intent.

The focus wand I will receive is a tool to help me form and command the energy with my mind. I had always wanted to learn how to transmute physical matter, and could hardly wait to start practicing, though I knew it would take many years to master.

For centuries, the Adani family had devoted itself to making focus wands. The Adani men belonged to an underground movement called the "Sacred Knights" whose purpose was to enlighten the people and keep the sacred work alive. The movement started several hundred years ago, but was forced to go underground when the Priest in those days decided he was the spokesperson for everyone's God. The men in this group risked their lives by making the wands, because the Priest ordained that only he had the power, and anyone else who claimed it had gotten it from the Gatekeeper, and was therefore an evil person, warranting death. As a result, anyone with paranormal abilities was considered a witch, and was in danger.

Before I received my gift of the focus wand I wanted to find a talisman to adorn it. A talisman is an uncommon object with mystical energy. I searched the woods, the lakeside, and all around our home for a suitable one, but nothing called out to me.

Best to keep at it, I reckoned, as I was running out of time. I hurriedly dressed and attended to my usual chores, then finished and set out on my adventure, heading out to the forbidden caves lying deep in the forest. The forest creatures kept the caves safe from those who would destroy the ancient pictographs on its walls. The Priest was known to send his guards in an attempt to destroy the evidence of our ancient ancestors who lived here.

As I walked through the woods towards the caves, something drew me to a group of trees. I felt the urge to pick at a piece of moss surrounding the base of a tall, majestic oak. I pulled back the moss, and there, wedged between two pieces of bark, found a piece of metal. I tried to pull it out, but it stuck. I pulled harder. It gave way all at once, releasing a metal ring, adorned with some type of stone, right into my hand. The stone was covered in dirt, so I was unable to tell its color. I turned it over and over in my hand. Then, holding the ring tight, I ran all the way home to tell my sister.

"Gwenneth, Gwenneth!" I shouted.

Gwenneth came out looking worried. "What's wrong?" she asked.

"I found it. I found my talisman!" I held it out for her to see.

"Where did you find this?" she asked as she picked it up.

"I found it in one of the oak trees."

She examined it closely while I excitedly babbled, "I found it! I found the talisman for my wand."

"Indeed you did," She looked down at me and smiled sweetly, as she always did whenever she was proud of me. That smile never failed to remind me I am loved and cared for.

A grand celebration had been planned for my thirteenth birthday. Birthdays have always been a festive time for us, a time to celebrate the gift of life. We would serve a sumptuous feast. Distant relatives would come to celebrate my special day. A festive robe was being made for me by my mother's sister, Aunt Kalini, who rarely visits because it's too risky. She is a powerful healer, well known by the townspeople, but thrown out of the town many years ago by the Priest who threatened to have her burned if he ever saw her again. I don't actually know the full story; no one will tell me.

But I remember her coming to visit around the time of my mother's death. Before she left, she bent down, looked me straight in the eyes and said, "You are a very special child. Your sister Gwenneth will protect you and keep you safe. Learn everything you can, be a good student of the sacred work, and the truth will free you. I will see you again when you turn thirteen." She hugged me tight, I pulled back and she looked at me with tears in her eyes, kissed my cheek, stood up, and walked away. That was ten years ago, and I was looking forward with considerable anticipation to seeing someone who knew my mother. I had a lot of questions about mother, questions only my aunt could answer.

Because we lived outside of town Gwenneth and I had the freedom to practice our sacred disciplines without being caught. Of course, living so far away had its disadvantages. We were not close to the town's marketplace. There were no other houses around ours, so I had no friends to play with, only our animals. There was a school in town established by the Priest and attended by children of different ages. How I wished I could go to school and make friends with the students. But Gwenneth wouldn't hear of it. "They won't accept you, you are different, and furthermore, you would not be welcome," she told me. "Besides, you are much smarter than they are because of your genetic line. You see how they look at us when we go into town once a month for our supplies."

It's true; I did see how they looked at us. Oh, it was fine to be smart and aware. But I was so lonely I was almost willing to give up all I knew, just to have friends. Sometimes, as I sat by the lake in my special place, I dreamed what it would be like to be a worshipper, to play with other children and have friends to laugh with, how it would feel to be like everyone else. Sometimes, when I heard the fairies, I pretended they were my friends. Since I didn't actually see them, it was easy to imagine what they looked like. I made the girls all have pretty long hair with beautiful dresses. I made the boys all handsome and wearing their finest outfits.

But my thirteenth birthday party would be different. Real people would be coming, and what a time we'd have! Gwenneth and I had been busy preparing for it. We cleaned the house and the outside garden area; cleaned the fire pit and stacked the wood in preparation for a great bonfire.

Musicians would be here to play their drums and wooden flutes all night long, so we could dance around the fire.

On the day before my birthday I made my way to the lake, removed my clothes and walked slowly into the water where I bathed with aromatic soaps I had never used before. I washed my hair with herbs my sister prepared for me, and it became almost as pretty as a town girl's.

Towards the end of the day people began to arrive. From the garden window I could see a tall man approaching from down our road. He wore a blue cloak; its filthy edge dragged along the ground. His long black beard touched his chest. I excitedly called out to Gwenneth to let her know a man was coming.

My excitement grew as I tried to guess who he might be. One of the Adani men? One of the musicians? A distant relative I never met? Gwenneth rushed to the door. I followed and stood behind her. She opened the door and stepped out to greet our first guest, and as he came closer I saw Gwenneth look at him quizzically. She stepped aside and allowed him to enter, then embraced him warmly. They hugged each other for a long time, and afterward held one another at arm's length for a better view. Finally, the man removed his cloak to reveal he was wearing a beautiful, ankle length dress. What a sight! A man in a woman's dress! Slowly his hand reached up to his face and removed the beard, wincing in pain. I could see his skin pull as the glue gave way.

"Shriya, it is I, your Aunt Kalini," the stranger announced.

Once the cloak was removed I could see and remember her wild, curly black hair, now flying every which way. She looked the same as she had ten years ago. I ran and embraced her as she bent down to hug me. She kissed me on each cheek and looked me in the eyes as she did back then. Her eyes were green like mine.

"You have become a very beautiful young lady. I understand you are progressing well in the sacred knowledge," she said.

"Yes," I answered. "I have studied well. I have studied the stars, geometry, and my inner sight is developing more and more as I do the sacred breath."

"Very good. Your mother would be proud of you." My heart jumped as she mentioned mother. If I hadn't known better, I would have immediately launched into questions, but I knew better than to ask them in front of my sister. Gwenneth would never allow it.

Gwenneth quickly started making tea, a customary courtesy to any guest. Not that we ever had guests. Well, an occasional traveler would stop by for a drink out of the well and a bite to eat...then no one for months. The women and children who showed up for healings were not guests. They came late at night and had no time for tea. Instead, we'd have to get right to work. Many of these visitors had to slip their husbands a special herb to get them to sleep quickly and deeply. It was the only way the wives could sneak out without their husbands knowing. All the women were familiar with herbs to keep their men sleeping for hours, but the men never knew. They considered herbs foolish, or thought the use of them was witchcraft. Either way, herbal magic was a woman's secret. Women had many secrets whether they were students of the sacred knowledge or lived as worshippers. It would have been detrimental to any woman's survival if a man of the town thought she had any real knowledge. Therefore, the town's women had to pretend they were worshippers, even if they didn't agree with the Priest. In that respect, my sister and I were fortunate, as our survival didn't depend upon any man. We were free to be ourselves as long as the Priest never found out about our healing abilities.

Chapter Three

Aunt Kalini and my sister were already sitting at the table drinking herb tea when I joined them. After a while, listening to them talk about things I didn't understand, I got bored. What interested me more was my aunt's jewelry. She had bracelets all up and down her arms, from her wrists to past her elbows. The one on her right forearm was a snake that coiled around her arm twice. The head of the snake had deep blue eyes that seem to penetrate into my own. It was a little unsettling, so I quickly glanced down at the rest of her bracelets. They were all metal, embedded with turquoise stones. Turquoise is said to bring good luck, as it wards off evil and is helpful for spiritual cleansing. Several of her bracelets had geometric designs which I recognized as sacred symbols with specific meanings.

Bracelets were only part of her adornment. She wore a ring on every finger except her thumbs. She must have loved turquoise because most of her rings were also embellished with it. So was her necklace of turquoise beads that dangled little metal charms, representations of nature. There were fir and pine trees, several suns, a few moons, little fairies and stars. The necklace took my breath away. Something about it made me smile inside.

In spite of enjoying the jewelry display, I was still bored and wished I were outdoors instead. Aunt Kalini must have sensed my uneasiness because she turned to me and said, "My dear, this is grown up talk and if

Gwenneth approves, you may be excused." I looked over at my older sister. She nodded her head. I wasted no time, in case either of them changed their minds. I hopped up, ran outside, and called Jumper, my wolf.

"Come, Jumper, come!" Jumper came as fast as he could. When running, he looked like a galloping horse trying to jump an obstacle. It's why he got his name. Jumper was a large wolf and weighed over five stone. He was not a watchdog. If I wanted one, I would have gotten a domesticated dog. I found Jumper when he was wounded as a wolf pup. He had fallen from a cliff and broken his leg. I went about healing him and once I had accomplished this, I left him to fend for himself. I was concerned his mother would come looking for him, and had no desire to be a she-wolf's dinner.

A year later I was sure I *was* going to be some animal's dinner! As I walked through the woods I sensed I was being followed, so I stopped, turned around, and there in front of me, not more than thirty paces away, was a gray wolf. He ran towards me at full speed. I stood frozen with fear. Before I could gather my wits, he lunged towards me. I dropped to my knees, covered my head with my arms and screamed in fear as the wolf landed on top of me. I felt his tongue lick my head and his nose nudge my arms. Then it dawned on me, this was the wolf pup I helped last year. As I wrapped my arms around his neck he tried to lick my face. I stroked his fur, rubbing both of my hands on either side of him. Unsure of what I should do next, I stood up and tried to walk away, but he followed me home and has been my pet ever since.

Like me, Jumper often wandered around in the woods. He'd come when I called him, but didn't actually have much interest in people, so when others came around he never paid attention. Anyone could sneak up on us without Jumper releasing so much as one howl. Nor did he pay attention to Gwenneth, who disliked him. But he disliked her, too, so they tended to ignore one another.

Jumper and I ran into the woods heading towards my special meditation place, but we both stopped at the entrance by two large evergreen trees. I trained Jumper not to enter my holy place without being asked. He liked to chase away the small animals I enjoy, so I didn't usually allow him to come with me. He'd either sit at the entrance and wait for me or run off and entertain himself. Sometimes he'd disappear for days at a time. He was a loner and loved to wander. But he could be very useful. I had no sense of direction, and got lost on several occasions, so I would only venture deep into the forest when he was with me. Jumper always knew how to get us home.

On the day before my birthday I wanted to be alone to think about what tomorrow would bring for me, so I left Jumper and made my way down the path to my holy place. I arrived at the lake in a solemn mood, trying to suppress the nervousness I felt about by birthday. I had never been to anyone's thirteenth birthday celebration, so I didn't have a clear idea of what to expect, or what would be expected of me. I closed my eyes and tried to imagine it. Nothing but anxious anticipation came. I hoped Parkin would be there to surprise me. Oh, how I longed to see him!

When I opened my eyes and looked out at the lake, I saw an eerie mist gather over the water. It slowly swirled and took on the form of a tunnel… one end touching the lake, the other open and facing me. I looked right into it and saw sparkling white lights bouncing around, when another form began to take shape in the middle of the tunnel. First there appeared to be a face, like the kind you might see when you look up at clouds. It got clearer as it slowly grew to become the image of a woman dressed in a long, flowing robe sparkling with the same dancing lights I saw earlier. The woman's face glowed with a light so bright I had to shield my eyes, and could not look at her directly. *"Shriya,"* I heard her say *"we are well pleased with you. Remember the ultimate ideal is to realize your own divinity. Never let your ego get the best of you."*

The image faded back into the lake as if it had never been. I didn't know what to think. Had I imagined it? I knew I didn't hear the misty woman's words with my ears, but they were clear as can be in my head. So many things confused me. I had many questions, but no answers. I gathered my thoughts and stood up, brushed myself off, and headed for home. Maybe Aunt Kalini would be able to help me with this experience.

I took my time walking back. Jumper was nowhere to be found, and I didn't call him. I preferred to contemplate my experience alone as I made my way home. What was the meaning of those words: "Never let your ego get the best of you," and, "We are well pleased with your progress." Who was well pleased with me? Who or what was it I saw?

When I walked in, Aunt Kalini was helping to prepare our evening meal. I asked if I might speak to her. She looked at me and noticed the concern on my face. She wiped her hands, sat down at the table and asked, "What is it Shriya? You look very upset." I sat directly across from her and told her about my experience. She listened intently and waited for me to finish before she replied.

"Shriya, do you understand the genetic line you come from?"

"A little. I know we are different and our ancestors have trained in the sacred arts for hundreds of years, and several have been killed by Priests because of what they knew."

"They were killed not because of what they knew; it was because of what they did. No one can know what you hold in your mind. Your thoughts are private and contained within your own consciousness. Only those highly advanced in studying the sacred work can perceive your thoughts. The Priests do not have that ability. So we are never persecuted for what we know, only for what we try to do because of what we know. Only when we act with that special knowledge does it become dangerous for us. For years, our family line has interfered with limited and closed minded thinking for the good of all mankind. There have been many times we have successfully changed events which prevented such things as the killing of innocent people. But sometimes our actions backfired and resulted in one of us being killed instead. When this happened, it was a true tragedy, because not only did we lose one of our own, but the Priest was able to go ahead with his plans. For us, interfering is a substantial risk, but the risk is much greater if we do nothing. Our lives are dedicated to making a difference. We also understand we will have the opportunity to come again and have another life, and are fortunate enough to have some recall of our previous lives. Each incarnation evolves us further, so each lifetime we have more and more memories from our past. However, our lifetimes may not be consecutive, one after the other, but parallel, existing at the same time."

She paused when she saw the confusion on my face. "Don't worry, Shriya," she smiled. "That subject is covered in advanced study, and you will be taught it only when you are ready. "

"But what does this have to do with what I saw this afternoon?"

"Did you not tell me the lady said, 'Never let your ego get the best of you?'"

"Yes."

"Sometimes it is very difficult to have knowledge others do not. We are a minority, and at times loneliness can almost consume us. There is a part of our inner self that wants so much to belong and fit in with others."

I could feel the tears wanting to come as I listened to my aunt. She had touched a chord in me, and I willed myself not to cry.

"But what is much worse," she continued, "is the desire to feel important. Self-importance is an attitude of our human personality. It is always lurking underneath our divinity waiting for a chance to get its way. It seems to me you are being given some type of warning. In the future you may be faced with a challenge your ego may want to control. You will need to be mindful of this. If you always keep the idea of service to others as your goal, it will keep your ego in check."

"I don't really understand this ego you are talking about. I have never given it any thought before, so it seems odd to me."

"It is because you are still a child coming into your adulthood. Once your body's energy starts to move down into your reproductive glands, your ego personality will become strong and make itself known. That change can be confusing. You may stop seeing dimensional beings like the ones you witnessed at the lake, and other realities may no longer be available to you."

"I saw a dimensional being?"

"Most likely. Her appearance was meant to give you some guidance for the future."

I sat and stared at her. I had never experienced anything like this before. After several minutes, I asked Aunt Kalini, "Why would I have this experience now, on the brink of becoming an adult, if adulthood will close the doors I already have to other realms?"

"I believe the experience came at this time so you will always remember the other realms. It is an experience you will not forget as you go into adulthood. It will help you keep your mind open to other possibilities. This is a grand thing, and you should be proud you have been found worthy enough to receive such an experience."

"Do you mean not every child turning thirteen has such an experience?"

"No, they don't. You must always remember you know more than most worshippers do. The knowledge and experiences given you are sacred and are never to be taken for granted."

A smile crossed my face as I realized how fortunate I truly was. I might have been lonely for human companionship, but I never lacked other-worldly experiences.

"I need to finish dinner; do you have any more questions, Shriya?"

"No. Not now." I got up and started to walk away when I had another thought, "Aunt Kalini?"

"Yes, dear?"

"Before you leave, I would like to talk to you about my mother. It's hard for me to remember her."

"Of course. I loved your mother very much. We were close growing up. I will be happy to answer any questions you have. But you must promise the conversation will remain between us. I don't want your sister to know I have shared anything about your mother with you."

CHAPTER FOUR

I FINISHED MY EVENING CHORES AND headed for the house where our dinner was probably ready. As I got closer, I could smell the halibut cooking over the fire. I loved fish, it was a special meal, only available in late spring and summer because the winters were too harsh for the men to go out in the boats. Actually, I loved all seafood, lobster being my very favorite. I had only eaten it once in my life because the Priest considered it trash, unfit to eat for any but the lowliest beings. You had to buy it directly from the fishermen, because it was never for sale in the market. Many years ago, on my sister's birthday, a gentleman came calling for her and brought three lobsters. I guess he liked them, too, and was trying to impress her. Apparently it didn't work with Gwenneth, but I was impressed. I never did understand why she wouldn't marry him. The only thing she would say was she didn't have room for a man; men only brought trouble. It seemed to me he brought lobster, and I didn't see what was so troubling about that.

As I walked into the house, I heard Gwenneth and Aunt Kalini laughing. They turned around as I walked in. "There you are," said Gwenneth. "You are just in time for dinner. Come, have a seat."

We ate well. Early spring greens provided a splendid salad. Often, when I was nervous, I couldn't eat. But on that night I ate as if I hadn't had a bite of food for a week. After, with a full stomach, I headed to the barn. Jumper had gone off earlier and was most likely running around chasing animals. I thought of calling him, but changed my mind. The sun was barely starting to set, and I was exhausted. All I could think of was how nice the hay bed was going to feel. On the few occasions when we had company, I got to sleep in the barn. There was no room inside the house. I liked sleeping outside and was happy to give up my space. I arranged my hay bed, settled down on it and closed my eyes.

The next thing I knew the sun was shining through a slat between two of the boards on the east side of the barn. Jumper had snuck in sometime during the night and lay at my feet. I had been in such a deep sleep I didn't hear him come in. rested quietly for a minute until I realized it was my thirteenth birthday. Then I jumped up with excitement, ran into the house and threw open the door.

"Good morning!" I shouted. Neither my aunt nor my sister were up. But at the sound of my voice, they both got out of bed yawning. Each came to me and held me tight for a long time.

"Today is a special day for you. So you may decide what we eat for breakfast. You may have whatever you want. It's your day, so it's your decision," Gwenneth said.

It was my day, and my excitement grew as I thought about my choices for breakfast. "Well," I said, "I think we should have eggs…with cheese on top, and some sausage." I know this was a lot to ask. We usually had tea and porridge, or whatever was still in the pot warming on the hearth and left over from the previous night.

"Whatever you like, Shriya. We will all share your breakfast bounty."

I went outside to gather fresh eggs and feed the chickens, goats, pigs, and Jumper. It was our custom for my sister to cook the food, but I took care of the animals. One of the pigs had already been separated from the rest, as he was to be butchered that morning, and roasted on an open pit during the day. By evening he will provide our feast.

I was so busy feeding the animals, I didn't notice two men coming down our road. By the time I looked up, they were almost at the door, ready to announce their presence. I stood and stared at their backs, and felt an uncomfortable flutter in the pit of my stomach. I figured they must be the

Adani men, as no other men were coming except the musicians, and I'd recognize them. Our families have known each other forever.

The men at the door were tall. One stood over six feet, the other was a bit shorter. My sister opened the door and greeted them with a deep bow, customary among those who study the sacred work. The men, in turn, bowed towards her. Although I had been taught good manners, I was nervous about meeting the men, and decided to finish feeding the animals and do all my morning chores before entering the house.

I deliberately took longer than usual to complete my chores, cleaning out the goat stalls with extra care. At that time of the year, the goats usually slept outside, so I didn't need to be cleaning the stalls at all, but I was trying to keep myself occupied for a time to calm myself down. Eventually, Gwenneth came looking for me.

"Shriya, company has arrived. I would like you to come inside so I can introduce you."

"Alright." I took a deep breath.

"Don't be nervous, Shriya. They have your best interests at heart. They are one of us, and excited to meet you."

"But I'm not used to being around men. I don't know how to be or what to say."

"You don't need to do anything other than simply be who you are."

We walked back to the house. When we entered, the men quickly stood up, clasped their hands together, placed them in front their heart, and slowly bowed towards me. I returned the bow. Our actions acknowledged the divinity in each other. It felt appropriate to greet one another this way, and it calmed me, a little.

"Shriya, this is Jabbar Adani. He is the father of Lusha Adani," Gwenneth said as she gestured towards his son. Lusha had curly, sandy blonde hair that hung down into his eyes. His hair reminded me of Aunt Kalini's. He had green eyes and a light brown complexion. His father, Jabbar, looked remarkably similar except his hair wasn't curly; it was the same color, but hung straight down to his shoulders. He had deep green eyes that looked right through you. Did Lusha's eyes do that? I looked back to find out. They were beautiful, but didn't have the same effect.

"It is a pleasure to meet both of you. Thank you for coming to my celebration," I said.

"We have been waiting a long time for this special day," Jabbar replied. "My son and I have been planning this for many years."

What a strange thing to say! Why would my thirteenth birthday be something they had planned on for years? But then again, I didn't know how men think, so I took it they didn't have much else to do in their lives.

I looked over at Lusha. He smiled a sheepish smile, blushed slightly and looked down at the floor. Men are odd.

"My son will be turning sixteen years old this year," Jabbar continued. "We will be celebrating his birthday, and will be honored if you and your sister are kind enough to join us."

I looked over at Gwenneth. Her face beamed as she replied, "We will be happy to. You will need to let us know the exact date so we will have time to prepare for the journey." I glanced over at Jabbar, and could swear I caught him winking at Gwenneth. But maybe it was my imagination.

"Come sit," Gwenneth said. "Let me put on the kettle for tea. Shriya, Kalini and I made biscuits for your arrival. Shriya, please go into the root cellar and bring a jar of strawberry preserve. Bring a jar of honey, also."

I was eager to leave the room. Something was going on I was not fully aware of. I didn't like the wink I'm sure I saw Jabbar give Gwenneth. Something was up, and I was determined to find out what. Gwenneth was a woman with many secrets, but I knew Aunt Kalini would be straightforward with me. I decided to ask her when I had the chance.

I went to the trap door which led to the root cellar, and carefully clambered down the steep steps. Whoever had dug the cellar made it almost as big as our house. It seemed like any other, but on its back wall there was a hidden door. The door was behind a large shelf containing mostly storage items such as large pots, pans, and extra trenchers. In front of the shelf, hiding the door, were several small casks of wine. More wine casks were arranged on other shelves along the wall.

Wine was a rare treat we drank only on spiritual occasions throughout the year. We still consider wine a gift from those who came before us. The grapevine is not native to our planet, but was brought to our world by beings from another star system. They planted it here so we could partake of the grapevine elixir during the summer and winter solstice. Wine drops the veil in our minds and lets us peer into the ether, permitting us to visit other levels of consciousness. It also allows us to see who we truly are. If we have any insecurities or hidden thoughts they will come out when drinking wine, as will any unconsciously suppressed emotions hidden in our soul. That's why the Priest forbade the drinking of it. He probably could not bear to see himself for who he actually was, nor would he want others in his control to be enlightened with the knowledge.

At that time, some of the townspeople had tried to create drinks from field grains, like the drinks sold in the ale houses. But the effects weren't the same. Grain potations destroy body cells, while red wine heals the physical body; the deeper the purple of the grape, the better its wine is for the blood's circulation.

When the current Priest gained control of the land, he burned all the local vineyards, including ours. I had never grown and harvested grapes nor processed them into the great elixir of wine. But we had many old recipes listed in books should future generations be able to grow grapes again. Until then it was illegal to grow them and too risky to try. Anyone caught growing grapes or making wine was immediately imprisoned. Was it illegal to have a wine supply? Maybe, but perhaps the Priest didn't know about ours.

The oldest wine we had was one hundred and seventy three years old. At some point before our vineyard was destroyed, we began to save two small casks of wine for every year. As a result, most of our wine is only ten to fifteen years old. The oldest wines were grouped with other relics of the past.

The holiest of all the relics were books of the sacred work which contain secret sciences of the universe, the story of creation, and much lost knowledge. Our family had the only set left. The rest were burned by previous Priests. These books were invaluable, and care of them was essential. We had a pivotal role to play in helping humanity realize the divinity living within them. We were not masters of the sacred work, merely students of it, with a broader perspective of life than the townspeople, most of whom were worshippers. They had to be, their life depended upon it. A worshipper would consider the idea of his own divinity blasphemous.

I grabbed the pot of preserve and looked over to my left for the honey. The honey supply was getting low. We only had two jars left. Honey was something we traded for at the market. One of the local worshippers raised honey bees and made some of the best honey in the country. Although the family would not trade with us directly, they sold to Janna's market, and she traded with us. Janna was wonderful to us. If it hadn't been for her, our lives would have been very different. She was well known and enjoyed a certain status in town, so she put up a front to fit in with the worshippers. But she had always supported us in every way. She knew everyone and heard all the gossip, including the facts if anyone was sick. She was invaluable to us.

I grabbed the honey and headed upstairs. It was awkward to climb back up with two jars held close to my chest. I didn't want to drop them; it would be embarrassing. Somehow I pushed the trap door open with my head and emerged inside the house. I produced the two jars and placed them on the shelf near the hearth.

"Thank you, Shriya. Please open them and place the sweets in serving bowls with the silver spoons." We had acquired a few dishes and were using them along with the usual serving trenchers because we had guests, or maybe because it was my birthday.

As the afternoon went on, others arrived. Some I had met before, when mother died. Others, I had never seen. Mostly it was women who showed up. A father and son arrived late in the afternoon, the last to come. They were the musicians who were to play that night at the bonfire. Again, my sister seemed to make a special fuss when introducing the son. Did Gwenneth forget I already knew him? This father also invited us to his son's sixteenth birthday, although Gwenneth didn't seem as interested in traveling to attend his celebration. Maybe they lived too far away. Yet, they were here, so apparently it wasn't too far for them to come to mine.

The atmosphere became very festive. The men gathered to tend the fire they built. It started out modestly, but as the afternoon progressed, they kept adding more and more wood to it. Jabbar went into the woods and hauled back a fallen tree. When he put the whole of it on the blaze everyone cheered.

I stayed by the fire while the men went off to slaughter the pig. I knew the men would say some type of prayer before they did it, but I had trouble watching any type of killing. Gwenneth often chastised me about my attitude. She liked to remind me I would starve if it weren't for her. That was not quite true, because I knew all the different plants, edible and poisonous, and was adept at distinguishing the mushrooms, as well. So I would have been fine if I never ate meat again. I could have survived on plants, herbs, and mushrooms. The land is plentiful, and I had been trained well on what can be eaten, what is used to heal, and what plants to avoid. But I liked the taste of meat. So, as long as I didn't have to slaughter anything, I'd continue to eat it, whether it was beef, pork or mutton, I liked it all.

The women were busy preparing the food, as I headed into the house to ask if I could help prepare anything. Gwenneth quickly looked my way as if I had startled her. "You go off and get yourself ready, put on your new dress and brush your hair. Then come over here, so we can see how wonderful you look."

"Really? Is it time for me to put on my dress?" I asked.

"Yes, it is time," Aunt Kalini chimed in.

I rushed off. My dress was a work of love made by Gwenneth, who was an excellent seamstress. It was very luxurious…made from silk, a rare and expensive cloth. Gwenneth saved for several years to buy the material. It was deep purple with a scooped neckline, long sleeves, and wrists cut at an angle. A braided blue cord wrapped around the hips. Aunt Kalini was by trade a jewelry maker and had created a necklace for me of polished mother-of-pearl beads, to compliment my new dress. She also included matching bracelet and earrings. The necklace and bracelet were single strands, but they were a treasure to me, since I had never owned jewelry like this. The earrings were more elaborate with three strands of beads, each as long as my little finger. I took my dress and hung it over the back of the clothes wardrobe door. I opened the pretty, carved box the jewelry came in and set it down on my set of drawers. I opened the top and took out my hair brush.

My hair was soft and thick, and since I had washed it the day before, brushing gave it a shiny, rich look. Yesterday I had also made an ornamental wreath to wear, searching the woods for the purple and blue flowers I loved and constructing it with forest green leaves, blue eyed grass flowers, and purple vetch. Now I put it on my head, looked at myself in our small looking glass, and marveled at what I saw. Not a child anymore, but a young woman looked back. A smile crossed my lips. I was indeed becoming a woman.

I peeked around the wooden screen that separated the sleeping area from the rest of the house, and when I was sure no men were present I walked out to where the women were working. My sister noticed me first and gasped, "Oh, Shriya, you are indeed beautiful." The other women turned and looked at me. My head swirled with excitement, nervousness, and anxiety, as I tried to hear what they were all saying, but their words jumbled together in my mind. Finally, Aunt Kalini came and put her arms around my shoulders and said, "Come and sit down, my dear. Have a cup of tea to calm your nerves."

I sat down and tried to drink some tea. My hand shook as I brought the cup up to my lips. I closed my eyes and said a silent prayer, "Beloved God, calm my nerves, fill me with peace and joy so that I may be present in your love during this great celebration."

I opened my eyes and felt peace flow through me. I knew I would be fine. I went back behind the screen. I had planned to wear the wreath at my birthday celebration, but noticed many of the flowers had fallen off, and others were faded and droopy. I didn't mind. My new silk dress and jewelry were ornaments enough.

Gwenneth came to me and let me know everyone was gathered outdoors. "Your guests have already lined up on both sides of the door to create a path for you to walk through toward the bonfire," she said. "Here are some herbs. They represent the transformation of your childhood into adulthood. You are to throw them on the fire. After that, turn and face your guests, and Lusha Adani will present the focus wand to you, another representation of growing into womanhood."

I nodded. I knew more would be expected of me in the future. "I'm ready," I said.

Gwenneth bent down and kissed my forehead. "Always remember to keep the focus. What you hold in your mind's eyes will become your reality. I love you, dear Sister, and I am very proud of you." She turned and went to join the others outdoors.

Proud of me? I never expected to hear her say those words to me. I wanted to cry, but then I thought of all the guests waiting outside. I didn't want my face stained with tears, so I quickly composed myself and walked towards the door. I stopped with my hand on the doorknob, said a prayer, and took a deep breath, "Thank you, my beloved God, for this day." Then I opened the door and started my walk into womanhood. I looked towards my right, and towards my left, and was thankful for all who came. I set my eyes on the fire and went into a light trance as I walked towards it. I could feel the energy rising warmly in my body. As I approached the fire, I took the herbs and threw them onto the fire. I turned and faced my guests. I had so much joy in my heart I smiled from ear to ear.

Lusha stepped out of the line and I could see a wand lying across his hands. He slowly walked up to me and bowed deeply. He held the wand towards me. "My lady," he said. "May I grace you with this gift? It is made with love and the blessing that you will do great things with it."

I looked down. My wand, adorned with a beautiful shiny, red ruby ring, glistened in the firelight. I took the wand from Lusha's hands and noticed how smooth and soft the wood felt. Geometric designs were carved all around it. I placed the wand against my forehead and allow my mind to meld with its beauty.

"Yes, I accept your gift. I thank you, and I promise I will make my genetic line proud." I lifted the wand and looked at all the people who had gathered to share this day with me. I wasn't sure what to do next when they all started cheering and clapping. Gwenneth came and took me by my hand. She led me to the house where I placed my beautiful wand on a shelf. I stood back and admired it, sure it would help me do marvelous things.

Then I hurried out to rejoin the party, still secretly hoping Parkin would show up and surprise me. I could not imagine having such a momentous day without him. It didn't seem right that he wasn't there. He is the one person I love as much as Gwenneth.

The musicians began to play and people started to dance. Lusha approached me and asked me to dance. I was a little apprehensive, but I agreed. The music has a lively rhythm, so he twirled me around and around. It was fun to dance in my new dress. For the first time in my life, I felt beautiful. The next song was slower. Lusha looked me in my eyes and said, "Will you do me the honor?" I hesitated, but I didn't want to hurt his feelings, so I nodded. It was uncomfortable being held close, but I closed my eyes and tried to imagine I was in Parkin's arms. Lusha seemed to be a pleasant and compassionate man, but he was not the love of my life. I was relieved when the music stopped.

"Would you like to enjoy some of the roasted pig?" Lusha asked.

"Yes, I would like that very much."

We walked over to where the pig, now nicely browned and smelling delicious, hung above the fire pit. The wood had burned down, but the embers were still red and hot. He cut off a hunk of meat and handed it to me. I took it from him and bit into it. It melted in my mouth. The way the fat oozed into the meat as it was slowly roasted made for a tasty meal. I could feel the juice dripping down my chin. I looked at Lusha smiling at me, wiped my face with the back of my hand and smiled back at him, but was uncomfortable when he didn't take his gaze off me. So I excused myself to look for my sister. I found her and Jabbar whispering about something. As soon as Jabbar saw me, he said loudly, "Oh, Shriya, come join us." Gwenneth tried to hide her surprise at seeing me. But I knew her better than that; I could tell I startled her. I wondered what she was up to.

As the evening went on, Lusha kept finding me and asking me to dance, or offering to get me a glass of wine. I didn't care much for wine, but I did love to dance. So I spent a lot of my evening with him. After all, there were few men to dance with. That didn't stop the other women; they danced with each other. Sometimes, they formed a complete circle around the fire and danced holding hands. Sometimes they even sang. Not me. I couldn't carry a tune, and I knew it. But Lusha sang with them every time. He was an excellent singer.

It was after midnight when I finally got ready to go to bed, but I was too excited to sleep. I went to the shelf to take another look at my wand and realized I could not leave it exposed. I retrieved my silk dress from the clothes cupboard and wrapped the wand in it, then placed the precious package in a bottom drawer. My wand was a sacred object. I knew I must guard it carefully. If it was ever discovered by the Priest, it would mean my life.

CHAPTER FIVE

I WOKE UP FILLED WITH ENERGY and jumped off of my bed of hay. "Good morning, sun," I said as I flung open the barn doors and went outside to greet the dawn. I went quietly back into the house to retrieve my wand, tucked the wand safely under my arm, and called Jumper. Together we walked towards the lake to my favorite meditation place. Jumper ran off to chase a squirrel. I wished the squirrel luck.

The sun was slowly rising over the mountain on that beautiful spring morning, and I was ready to start my wand exercises. There was a small rock in front of me. I decided to transmute it into a piece of gold, and buy something special for Gwenneth with it. Then wouldn't she be proud of me! I got comfortable, set my wand across my lap and closed my eyes. I let my mind slip into an altered state of consciousness. As my body relaxed, my mind continued to go deeper and deeper. I stayed in this state until I felt power surge within me. I opened my eyes, stood up, and pointed the wand directly at the rock. I visualized the rock turning to gold. I could feel the power building in me, coming down my arm and out the tip of the wand towards the rock. But nothing happened. The rock remained a rock. I tried not to be discouraged, and repeated the process. Again…nothing. "Well, that's enough of wand exercises for one day," I said, as I got up and left, annoyed with myself and embarrassed by my failure.

On the walk home I called Jumper. He came running so fast he almost knocked me over in his eagerness. I bent down and hugged him, my best companion, and found comfort there, but was still disappointed about my failed focus exercise. I honestly expected something more. I wanted the rock to at least quiver slightly as I tried to transmute it. Jumper licked my face. I hate that! But it lifted me out of my bad mood. Good wolf.

When I got home, Gwenneth was nowhere in sight, so I went down to the cellar to read the sacred books. I looked up "Transmuting". As far as I could tell, I did everything correctly. I decided to try again the next morning.

Satisfied, I went outside to sit near the garden and enjoy the flowers. All of a sudden, a swarm of bees came at me with such intensity I thought they were going to attack. Instead, they circled around me several times, then created a pathway in the middle of the air that led to one of the trees. They wanted me to follow them! I did, and found their hive had fallen out of the tree onto the ground. The queen had not left her hive, but the other bees were concerned about her. I ran to fetch my gloves, and reinstalled the hive back to its original place. The bees once more circled around me, and I felt a warm and invigorating energy surround my body. "You're welcome," I said silently. The bees entered their hive where they were safe and secure. At such times I felt most alive. I turned to see Gwenneth, who witnessed the entire process. She smiled at me, and beckoned me back to the house. "Breakfast is ready," she said.

In the evening, after dinner was over and the area cleared and tidy, Gwenneth brought bunches of different herbs to the table, to be used for healing joint pain. An older woman was coming that night for a healing. I wanted to stay and watch but could hardly keep my eyes open. Our spring nights can be cold, so Gwenneth built a fire in the fireplace. The cozy warmth put me to sleep in a fireside chair. A knock on the door awoke me around midnight. I rose and opened the door to find Janna and one of the older women from town. She was probably in her sixties, and her gnarled hands revealed a story of pain and suffering. She limped in, barely able to move, and explained that her inability to walk at a normal pace caused them to arrive late.

I called out to Gwenneth, "Our visitors are here."

Gwenneth appeared. "Good evening, Janna, good evening, Ma'am."

The woman smiled at both of us. "I am in a lot of pain and can hardly move about my house or perform my wifely duties," she said. "This makes my husband very angry. Can you help me?"

I opened my mouth to protest, but Gwenneth glared at me… a warning to keep my mouth shut. I took a deep breath in order to swallow all the words wanting to fly out.

Gwenneth remained calm. "Come, let's see what we can do," she said, as she guided the woman toward our healing area and had her lie down on the treatment table.

The treatment table was designed for healing the sick. Its bed was waist high because we usually stand when we work, sometimes for hours if the problem is chronic and we need to rearrange the patient's cellular structure. The table was made of oak and is hundreds of years old. It had been in our family for many generations, and served us well.

There was an old story of its origins. In those ancient times, in order to take a tree's life there had to be mutual agreement with it. Most trees, even today, outlive humans by hundreds of years and hold the memories of many generations. A tree will tell you the historical stories of the human life it has witnessed if it feels you are worthy. Anyway, the people who created this table did a trance dance before they set out on their journey to find the right tree. During this ceremony they wore masks made of bark, leaves, moss, and other natural materials representing the energy of a tree. They danced for hours to insure the perfect tree would make itself known to them.

At that time, ancient celestial beings were still here on our planet. When the dancers completed their dance, the celestial beings took them into the forest to find the perfect tree. As they made their way, a large oak tree fell across the path right in front of them. They cheered and praised Mother Nature for providing them the material they needed. The tree had given up its life in order to be a healing table that was strong, resilient and hardy.

We bent over the table, Gwenneth at the woman's head, and I at the woman's ankles. I removed her boots, and saw her toes were as gnarled as her fingers. I closed my eyes and allowed myself to go into a trance. My energy was erratic, not free-flowing. I opened my eyes, and noticed a faint light around the woman's body. At first it was white, but soon it began to change colors, turning from yellow to green and back to yellow again. It was the first time I had ever seen a light around someone's body. I knew her cells were older and broken down from stress, fatigue, and an overuse of emotions. I wondered if the colors I saw around her came from them.

I closed my eyes again and focused on health until Gwenneth broke my trance by reciting a blessing. "Beloved God, bless this woman, heal her body that it may know youth and joy again. So be it."

I looked up at my sister, and we smiled at each other. I was tired and ready for bed, but Gwenneth still had to administer herbs to the woman, so I moved away to let her do it. The woman would need some time to rest before she can travel home.

I returned to my chair and quickly fell asleep. I woke up when I heard Janna and Gwenneth help the woman out the door. She looked better and seemed more agile than when she first arrived. I was glad they were leaving. I wanted nothing more than to sleep. Gwenneth shut the door behind them and said to me, "The healing is not over. We must continue it as she makes the long trip home. It is important for her to arrive there before her husband wakes up. I will wake up your aunt and ask for her assistance. We will need all the help we can get tonight."

"Tonight?" I groaned. All I could think of was going to sleep.

"Yes, Shriya. I know you are tired, but it must be tonight. And we should start right away." She bustled about, and found a scrap of paper she had saved and a small piece of graphite. She handed them to me and said, "Draw!"

I drew an outline of a smiling, healthy woman, placed the picture against my forehead and secured it with a headband. Then Gwenneth, Aunt Kalini and I went outside and built a fire. Once it was ablaze, I let the flames put me in a light trance. Gwenneth, too, stared into the flames, as she beat a drum rhythmically. Aunt Kalini began to dance around the fire. I stood up, closed my eyes and began to dance, too. As I danced, I held the image of the woman's body in perfect health. We were prepared to do this dance for her every night until she was better. Or every morning. The veil between the two worlds was always the thinnest at the earliest morning hours, making it the best time to try and change anything in the etheric field.

We barely made it to bed before the sun came up. Luckily I had done my morning chores before going to sleep. When I awoke I could tell by the sun's position it was past noon. I dressed in a hurry and headed straight to my meditation place to start wand practice again, determined not to give up. I spent the next three years practicing, but never did transmute that stone.

Chapter Six

March 15, 1543

WE WERE GETTING READY FOR another birthday celebration. In a month I would be sixteen, a birthday that marks another significant point in our lives' work. Gwenneth and I liked to go out of our way to make each other's birthdays special. The birthday girl decided what the other one would fix for dinner. I always asked for lobster. I never got it, but I asked for it anyway, and usually settled for fish. Our everyday meals consisted mostly of grains, beans both dried and fresh, vegetables, and fruit in season. Because we raised pigs, goats and chickens, we could liven our daily fare from time to time with the meat of the animals we slaughtered. Occasionally, we'd eat beef. There are several families in the area who raise cows, so the market had plenty of it, but it was expensive.

We always made some type of sweet dessert on our birthdays, a rare treat as sugar was hard to come by and very expensive. Our birthdays are seven months apart, giving us plenty of time to plan and save.

Whenever we went into town for fish, I got excited in the hope of seeing Parkin, and several times I did. Of course, Gwenneth would not allow me to talk to him or even talk about him. One day I saw him on his boat, so I stared at him from a distance hoping he would sense someone was looking at him. Gwenneth caught me staring in his direction and scorned me for it. She knew what I was doing, and she didn't want me to attract his attention. The next month I saw him again, and he came right up to us and started a conversation, but Gwenneth quickly made up some excuse as to why we had to leave. She was determined to keep him away from me. The more it became apparent she didn't want me to be around him, the more I wanted to. I couldn't get him out of my mind.

We had an earthenware flour container in the kitchen, and besides flour, we kept our coins in it. Gwenneth would wrap the coins in a piece of cloth and place the packet at the bottom of the jar. Every month when she added more coins, she created a big mess yet she never changed the location. She said it was a safe place because no one would ever think to look inside of it. Flour was inexpensive and abundant, and like most of the households in town, we used a lot of it.

I loved to bake and would produce two or three loaves of bread a week, as well as biscuits. We had biscuits almost every morning, and bread at every meal. Baking was my job, but I was only allowed to bake sweet treats once every few months, or for special occasions like birthdays. I'd usually try a new recipe using honey first. If it didn't taste good, at least I hadn't wasted sugar. Generally, though, I had more successes than failures. I had a natural knack for it.

"Shriya, after dinner I would like to speak with you. We need to talk about your sixteenth birthday coming up."

"Okay, Gwenneth," I replied. There wouldn't be the fuss for this one as there was for my thirteenth, but I had a funny feeling there was going to be more than my birthday to discuss. My Aunt Kalini would probably come to help us celebrate, but as far as I knew, no one else would be there. After dinner, Gwenneth and I sat outside in the spring air and looked up at the stars.

"Do you remember meeting Lusha Adani when you turned thirteen?" she asked.

"Of course. We visited him and his father for his sixteenth birthday celebration."

"What did you think of Lusha?"

"What do you mean, what did I think of him?"

"Well, you are almost sixteen -- time to think of your future. It is part of our responsibility to continue our genetic line."

A horrible feeling rose inside of me. I didn't like where this conversation was going. I could feel myself becoming pale and weak. I didn't know what to say, so I just glared at her.

"Shriya, don't look so distraught. Certainly you knew this time would come. Haven't you given any thought about marrying and having children? You are at that age where most young women start courting with the intent to marry a young man and start a family."

"No, Gwenneth, I haven't. You're not married, nor do you ever talk about marrying. I have always assumed you and I would live together alone since you won't even let me speak to Parkin. I don't have any plans to marry any more than you do, unless it's to him. I have no desire to leave you."

"My dear," Gwenneth said, as she reached over and placed her hand on mine, "We must talk about the idea of marriage for you. It is important you bear a child to carry on the sacred work. We must all do our part. It is our heritage to fulfill this promise to God and humanity."

I pulled my hand away. "Why me? You are the older sister. You have never borne a child nor have you ever had any interest in any of the men who came around here wanting to court you!" I could feel my face redden as the words flew out of my mouth. "Parkin, by the way, is not a worshipper. He is a fisherman from a tribe. As for the young men from town, you never even let me speak to any of them. You led me to believe I was not allowed to be married. Yet now you tell me I must. This is so unfair!" I shook my head in disbelief and anger.

"Shriya, I understand your anger and confusion, but there is a reason I have remained unmarried all these years. Before now, I felt you were too young to understand, but you have grown and matured, so I am ready to discuss it with you this evening."

"Fine. Talk. I'm listening," I said.

"This is difficult. It's something I have tried to forget, and yet it lives with me every day," she began.

I saw her eyes tear up, and that concerned me deeply. Gwenneth never showed emotion. She was always matter of fact about things. The last time I saw her cry was when our mother died. As soon as I saw her tears, my attitude changed. I leaned towards her in an effort to show I cared and was listening.

Gwenneth continued, "When I was sixteen, in the middle of summer on a very hot day, I walked alone back from town. When I arrived home, hot and sticky, I decided to take a swim in the lake. I was used to living around nature and the freedom of it. Our father died when you were only a toddler and I, a young girl. In our all female household I was never taught to be modest and was innocent about my body. It never occurred to me someone might watch me with ill intent."

"Gwenneth, what are you saying?"

"I am saying a man from town followed me, and I was not aware of it. I was taking off my clothes when I was attacked. He came up behind me and dragged me around the back of a big rock. He abused me in a way I do not want to repeat out loud, nor do I want to remember. But my female organs were damaged and I am unable to carry a child."

I looked at her, stunned and speechless. I finally mustered a whisper, "Sister, I don't know what to say. I am shocked. How horrible that must have been for you."

"More than horrible. I do not understand why this happened. But I did not take the time to look into the future, so I did not see it coming. I live with this guilt and shame every day."

"But why do you blame yourself?" I said. "The shame should be with the man who hurt you. You taught me we are not always aware of what may come into our lives. I don't think you should feel guilty."

"Shriya, I know you are right, but I expect more of myself. I became careless and neglected to look into the future on a daily basis. As a result, I jeopardized our genetic line. That is why I rarely miss a day of seeing the future. In order to change it, I must be able to see the time line."

I didn't understand. "Time line? What's that?"

"A time line is a future you are aligned with, one your accumulated thoughts and actions have brought into your life. However, once you look down that time line and see what is coming into your life, you have the option of changing it. You can go into a trance and alter the future. You can change the reality to anything you want. But I became lazy and stopped looking. I was caught up with the feelings of being in love and forgot what was important."

"You mean the one you were in love with did that to you?"

"Oh, no. He would never have hurt me. I was deeply in love and betrothed to him. He was from the ancient royal line of the Sacred Knights, a proper order that studies the sacred work. He was older than I, but I didn't care. The ten years difference didn't seem important. As soon as I met him, I felt I had known him all my life. And I felt fortunate I would be able to carry on the sacred lineage and marry someone I loved. So much of our history records women marrying only for the sacred work.

As I listened to Gwenneth, I saw stars in her eyes as she talked about her fiancé. But as she continued her story, the look changed to extreme pain, and her eyes welled with tears.

"In one afternoon it was all torn from me. The marriage was off. Since I could not have children, I was no longer marriage material. So, I not only suffered severe physical pain, but I also had to carry the burden of the intense emotional pain of losing the man I loved. My dream life was over, just like that."

I went and retrieved a handkerchief for her, to wipe her running nose and the tears streaming down her face. I had never seen her in such distress before. I understood her grief, but didn't know what to do about it, so I just handed her the handkerchief, put my arms around her and cried with her.

It took some time before Gwenneth regained her composure. "Now you see, Shriya, why it is up to you to continue our genetic line and continue the sacred work. You must marry, become pregnant, and raise the child to carry on with it. The future of humanity needs us. It is up to us to help change the energy field so the consciousness of humanity has a chance to evolve into a greater reality."

"Why is it up to me? I am not powerful enough to change humanity's consciousness. Gwenneth, you put too much faith in me. I am a young woman with no real power."

"You are now almost sixteen, and old enough to consider marriage. Every person is more powerful than he or she realizes. Every thought and action affects the energy field. The more focused your intent, the more powerfully your thoughts affect this field. You have been trained well, and your intent affects this energy field more than you know. With additional training you will have the ability to change the direction of humanity. It is your responsibility to do so."

"But I don't want that responsibility!"

"It is not an option. You made the choice to incarnate into this genetic line, you agreed upon this before your birth," Gwenneth said.

"I did not agree. I have free will!" I screamed. I could feel myself become more and more enraged.

"Of course you have free will. But I also know you will make the right decision. You are not a selfish person; I have not raised you that way. Shriya, calm down. I am not trying to upset you, but you need to understand what will now be expected of you."

My feelings spiraled down to a place where I didn't want to go. If I allowed it, I might have trouble coming back. I couldn't afford to lose control. I took a deep breath, closed my eyes, and silently asked God for guidance.

"My beloved God, give me the strength to see this situation clearly. Cleanse my mind so I can respond appropriately." I kept my eyes closed for several minutes, and tried to push the thought of Gwenneth out of my mind. I needed to stay open for guidance. Then I heard her sigh. Oh, no! I didn't want to hear what she was doing. Before I could think, I sensed a loving energy fill my body and a deep peace flow inside of me. I took another breath and opened my eyes.

"Gwenneth, I need time to absorb this conversation," I said. "You told me a lot tonight. You opened your soul to me and shared a deep hurt that still causes you great pain. I am honored you felt safe in sharing your experience with me, and I realize it was still extremely difficult for you to tell. It explains some things about you I never understood, like why you were never interested in any of the men who showed an attraction to you. I took your attitude to mean that you and I would never marry or leave each other. But now you are asking me to change, and to consider marrying a man I don't love. Honestly, Gwenneth, I have thought about what it would be like to have a child, but I never allowed myself to fully dream that dream."

I wasn't being totally honest with her. For months I had been dreaming and doing the trance dance to create Parkin in my life.

Gwenneth shook her head. "Oh, Shriya, I don't want you to pattern your life after mine. I want you to be happy, marry a wonderful man, have children, and continue the sacred work. My life has not been a happy one." She must have caught the look on my face, because she quickly explained, "I have enjoyed raising you and am very thankful for your innocent outlook on life. You have brought great joy to my life, but it does not replace the desire to have a husband and to bear children of my own."

"I understand. But where do you expect me to find a husband?" We both knew the town was filled with worshippers, and she would never allow me to marry one, for that would put an end to our genetic line. Besides, no male worshipper would tolerate a woman who realized the power of the divine was in everyone.

"Let's talk about the Adani family again"

"They gave me my focus wand."

"Jabbar is the young man I was in love with."

"Jabbar?"

"Yes, Jabbar Adani was my fiancé many years ago."

"But I heard he has a wife who is very ill and bedridden."

"Yes. She is paralyzed. Her name is Oma, and she is from a genetic line of distinguished healers. Her grandmother was burned at the stake for being a witch. Oma's mother, Jina, suffered greatly at the loss of her own mother. Jina blamed the sacred work for the death of her mother. So she swore never to practice the sacred work or any of the healing arts again. You see, although Oma is from a strong genetic healing line she was never taught any of it. Genetics don't necessarily do any good without the education and knowledge. Oma does not accept that she can heal herself, nor will she allow anyone to heal her. Once I was deemed no longer eligible to be married, Jabbar was sent off immediately to marry Oma. There wasn't anyone else with the proper genetic lines for him to marry. Jabbar and Oma had one child... Lusha."

Oh, my God! The thought came to me before she even said it. She wanted me to marry Lusha! Lusha, her ex-fiancé's son. This could not be happening. This was a nightmare.

"Lusha? You can't possibly be serious. I barely even know him. Why is Lusha acceptable and Parkin is not?" I demanded an explanation, but the truth was, I already knew the answer but wanted her to say it, because I was having a hard time comprehending I could end up in an arranged marriage.

"Lusha would make a perfect genetic match for you," she said calmly. "Lusha is a nice young man. I thought you two got along well when we went to his sixteenth birthday celebration."

"Yes, we did, as friends. But I had no idea you were planning to marry me off to him!" By now I was furious. How could she betray me like this? How could she not have told me about her inability to conceive and have a child? How could she have kept such a secret all these years, especially when it affected me?

"Gwenneth, I will not let you do this to me. I tell you now, I will not marry any man but Parkin! I jumped up from the table and ran out the door, ran down the road and continued to run towards town.

I ran and ran as tears burned my face, not paying attention to where I was going, until I finally stopped at the edge of town.

The sun had almost set, the sky was already darkening. I bent over, out of breath, my head spinning, my tears still raining down. I fell to my knees and cried from the depths of my soul. I felt betrayed by my own sister. She had this planned all along and never told me. The one person I thought I could always trust had lied to me all these years.

I had never been this close to town by myself, and was always expected home by sunset. I looked in the direction of the docks, but was too far away to see the boats. I wondered if Parkin was in the area. Maybe if I went a little farther down the road, I'd be able to see if his boat was there. I realized I had an unexpected opportunity to see Parkin alone, without Gwenneth there to take me away. My excitement rose at the anticipation of possibly seeing him tonight. I had to try, even if it was getting dark. Even knowing it was dangerous for an unaccompanied woman, especially an outsider like me.

I was afraid to proceed, but my desire was stronger than my fear, so I moved forward. I watched for any movement that might alert me to nearby danger. Because this is a seaside town, a lot of men travel here, bringing goods from other parts of the world. It was rumored that the ale house women serviced a man's needs. But I had heard talk that some of the men forced themselves on unsuspecting women. Such a man attacked and raped my sister. I shuddered as I thought of that horrible day for Gwenneth, and tried to put it out of my mind because I needed to stay focused on my desire to see Parkin.

I was sorry Gwenneth's life had been disrupted, but I didn't see why it had to ruin mine. So if Gwenneth wanted me to marry, then maybe I would run away and marry Parkin. In fact, I had run away. I didn't have to go back. I could find Parkin and tell him how my sister wanted to arrange a marriage for me. I imagined him begging me not to marry Lusha. He would take me in his arms and kiss me passionately, telling me how much he loved me. We would run away together and live with his tribe. I could still continue my sacred work. I'm sure the tribesmen would accept me. After all, the Priest did not approve of them either. We would have that in common. If Gwenneth expected me to marry someone I didn't even know, I would run away and marry Parkin.

CHAPTER SEVEN

I HEADED FOR THE DOCKS AND looked for Parkin's red and blue boat. The wear and tear on it told its history; it was old but well used. I walked up and down the docks in search of a glimpse of Parkin or his boat, but had no luck. Festering in me was a deep urge to teach Gwenneth a lesson. I wanted to run away with Parkin to show her I had control over my own life. She needed to know I was not to be bartered for her beliefs.

It was getting hard to see, and I worried about being out so late. I didn't want to go home, but I had nowhere else to go. Neither friends nor family lived close by. Defeated, my only choice was to turn around and make my way back.

I was confused. Part of me was distraught over what my sister had experienced. But another part was concerned only with how it affected me. It was a dark night by the time I neared home, where candle light flickered invitingly in one of the windows. I halted at the beginning of the road that led to our house, looked up into the sky and silently prayed. "Beloved God, be with me during this troubled time. Give me the guidance I need to respond appropriately."

I walked to the front door, paused, took a deep breath, and opened it. Gwenneth was still sitting at the kitchen table. Her eyes were stained with tears and her face was red from crying. As I looked at her, my heart sank.

She looked so vulnerable. How could I be selfish? How could I not honor her request after what she had been through? I pulled the other chair out and sat down.

"Sister," I said. "I am so sorry your dream was destroyed. I wish you had told me many years ago. I would have understood why you have always been so reserved."

"Shriya, I have always loved you," she said softly. "Having you in my life has kept me going. My job has been to protect you from the ill will of people until you were old enough to understand not all of them have good intentions. I did not want you to grow up afraid, and that has created a difficult balance for me. When you first came home and told me about your experience looking into the lake and seeing a future vision, I knew it was a message not only for you, but for me, as well. I wanted to say, 'Never go to the lake. Bad things can happen!' But if I had allowed my fears to prevent you from enjoying the lake and the woods, it would have stunted your own spiritual growth.

So I committed to look into the future every day. I made you the object of my focus so I could see if any harm was going to come your way. That is why on some days, I'd keep you near me here at home by giving you extra chores, or extra studies from the sacred books. There were also times when I saw something happen to you, tried to alter it, but it happened anyway, usually because of your stubborn insistence on behaving as you wished."

I had to smile. "I thought you were the stubborn one, Gwenneth, not me."

Gwenneth laughed. "Oh, my dear, you are just as stubborn as I. We get it from our mother. You see my stubbornness because it is a reflection of yourself."

She was right. We were both stubborn. I was just more subtle about my stubbornness than she.

"Come here, Shriya." She opened her arms wide to embrace me.

I hesitated to hug her. I wasn't ready to admit defeat. I still felt I had the right to refuse her marriage idea, so I said, "Sister, I will consider your idea, but that is all I agree to for now. I do not like the idea at all. The idea of leaving you terrifies me. I have no wish to leave our home. It is my home, and I intend to stay in it. But in fairness, I will consider everything you said tonight. It is important for me to make a wise decision, and I will give it to you in a few days."

"That is fair, Shriya. You are not bound to continue our genetic line, even though I believe that was an agreement you made on a soul level before you incarnated into this lifetime. However, we all have free will and have been given the right to make our own choices."

Guilt. She was going to use guilt to get her way. "I'm going to bed now, Gwenneth," I said. "I've had more than enough to deal with in one evening."

I went to bed physically and emotionally exhausted. My body ached everywhere from stress and I could not sleep. I kept going over Lusha's sixteenth birthday party in my mind. They lived a full day's walk away. We got up early, ate breakfast, packed a lunch and headed towards the east. It was beautiful to watch the sun slowly rise and move across the heights as we made our way along a river that cut deep into the mountains. Deeper still, we would find the Adani family, who had settled many years ago in a small, but charming village set like a jewel in a broad green valley.

It was a tiring walk, and we were happy to stop for lunch at high noon. We found a large tree to provide us some shade as we enjoyed our meal of home baked bread, tangy cheese, carrots, and pickled cabbage. The bread had lost some of its freshness but when you're hungry, everything tastes good.

We arrived as the sun was setting. Jabbar was happy to see us. Lusha stayed back in the shadows, and I wondered why he was acting so shy. He must have known about the plan to marry us and thought I was naïve and foolish when Gwenneth kept nudging me to talk with him.

I don't know how long I kept running those memories through my head, but at last I fell asleep. The next morning when I got out of bed, I found Gwenneth, still sitting where she had been the night before. "Gwenneth, didn't you go to bed last night?" I asked.

"No, I didn't. My mind was racing, and I sat awake for most of the night. When I did drift off, I had a dream we would have a visitor today. Janna is bringing a child to us, a girl about three years old suffering from food poisoning. She is the granddaughter of the Priest, and they are coming in the middle of the day."

"How can that be? The Priest would never allow it to happen. If it is true and the little girl comes, we will be condemned to death if we heal her and he finds out."

"I think we will be safe," Gwenneth replied, "I understand your concern, but she is an innocent little girl. The cells in her body will hold the memories of health, and food poisoning is relatively easy to cure. I believe they are on their way now. "

Gwenneth got up and began to prepare the herbal remedy to flush out poison from the child's body. I prepared our treatment area. I burned a cleansing herb to clear out any negative energy, and lit several candles. I put one of the blankets near the fire to warm it up. It wasn't long before Janna arrived carrying the sick child wrapped in a blanket.

Janna was in her middle thirties, fair skinned, with waist-length black hair which was most often seen in a bun high on top of her hair. She was fairly tall for a woman, and a little pudgy, but remarkably beautiful. Her skin was so light, the gossips in town whispered she was from an old royal race, but no one could say for sure if the rumor was true.

Janna was always well dressed, even when she brought people to us in the middle of the night, and her dresses were beautiful. Many were made of silk. There was a seamstress in town, but only the very wealthy could afford to have their clothes custom made by her. The seamstress made all of the Priest's robes. He wore silk robes adorned with gold and silver embroidery for his weekly lectures. Janna had all her dresses made by the seamstress and some of hers had embroidery, as well. Owning the market was a profitable business. Although Janna and her husband had a lot of money, they were very humble, and made it their mission in life to aid others. Whenever anyone fell on hard times, they did what they could to help. Sometimes it was by extending credit to a family, sometimes giving away extra food they had on hand.

I looked at the little girl Janna was holding. She was dressed in silk. I wondered if she would grow up to be like Janna or become a self-righteous woman. Gwenneth interrupted my thoughts.

"Please bring the child over here," she told Janna, who followed Gwenneth to the treatment area.

"And you, Shriya, bring the herbal medicine quickly!"

I brought it around. It smelled bad and I wondered how we were going to get the child to drink such an unpleasant concoction. I set it down nearby.

Janna moved off to allow my sister and I to start the process. Janna loved children, all of them, perhaps because she couldn't have any of her own. Several years ago I heard her asking Gwenneth for a medicine to make her fertile. Gwenneth sent her home with several flasks of potions, but advised her the problem could be with her husband. If the fertility problem was not Janna's, then a different medicine would need to be prepared for him. After about six months Janna came asking for the man's medicine. Gwenneth and I prepared herbs to improve the male reproductive system. But still, after several years, Janna remained childless. I guess some people weren't meant to have children of their own. Janna's gift was in being a mother to others.

As we got ready to work, Gwenneth began to tell me about our little patient. "Her name is Christina.

She is Janna's niece. This is Alyssia's daughter." Alyssia was Janna's younger sister. She married the Priest's son, Devon, when she was eighteen years old, and had this child within the first year of their marriage.

Christina looked nothing like her mother or aunt. Her resemblance was to the Priest's family line. But the most important thing at the moment was how pale and sickly she looked. Her eyes were closed and she was covered in sweat as her body tried to rid itself of the poison.

Sorry as I was for her, I was equally concerned about the dangerous situation her illness had created for Gwenneth and me. She was the Priest's granddaughter. If she died while she was here, we would be blamed for killing her. If we were able to save her, we risked the chance of being burned for witchcraft. I closed my eyes as Gwenneth started a prayer. "Beloved God, be with us as we align ourselves with your love. Allow the powerful healing energies of your divine will to flow through us and heal this precious child. Give her the long life she deserves."

"So be it," we said in unison.

I held Christina's feet, and could feel Gwenneth's energy scan the child's body to find where the poison was striking the hardest. We found her energy was weakest at her stomach and spleen. Food poisoning attacks the stomach first, then the spleen has to work overtime in an effort to fight off the food's poisons. Usually a body will purge itself by vomiting, diarrhea, and perspiration. Food poisoning isn't always life threatening, especially for an adult. But a child's system is so fragile, even a mild case can kill. Luckily, we were able to cleanse Christina's body by a laying on of hands over the affected organs and getting the herbal medicine down her throat. She was so sick she showed no resistance to swallowing it.

Afterward Gwenneth, Janna and I sat down at the kitchen table.

"She will be fine," I said. "Let her rest here for another hour before you return home. Her body needs time to adjust to the treatment we gave her."

"Thank you," Janna said with great relief. "I was so worried, and so was my sister. Alyssia feared God was angry with her, and showed it by making her child sick."

"Why would God punish an innocent child?" I asked.

Janna looked at me and said, "Alyssia had a fight with her husband, Devon, over a lecture his father, the Priest, gave last Sunday. He said women were not equal to men, and should obey their husbands. Alyssia took offense at this and told her husband so. Of course, Devon agreed with his father. What man wouldn't want to have control over his wife if he allowed it?"

"A man of the sacred work would never want to control another, be it his wife or his neighbor. He would understand God's love resides in every person, which makes everyone equal in God's eyes," I said with great conviction. Secretly I wondered if my words were true or if I only hoped they were.

"Well, that may be, but a worshipper isn't going to admit women are divine," Janna said, laughing.

I didn't see the humor in it, but Gwenneth laughed with her. I had to ask, "Are you saying that if God does not agree with what she said, God would make her innocent child sick?"

"That's her concern." Janna responded.

"Putting the fear of God in people works well doesn't it?" I asked.

"Yes, it does. It's a sad thing, but strong emotions can paralyze people into submission. They are afraid of what will happen when they die. They have been told if they displease their god, they will be sent to the underworld of evil for all of eternity. However, sometimes emotions will compel a person to act contrary to what they have been taught is wrong. They will stand up for their beliefs regardless of the consequences. But that is rare indeed."

I looked at Janna and had to ask, "Why aren't you consumed with fear like the rest of the worshippers?"

"There is a long lineage of royalty in my family. When the Priest's family took over, most of my ancestors were condemned to death. At one time it was said a celestial royal race from beyond the North Star came and seeded this planet. There are ancient drawings of them in the caves. My family line is said to be from this race. These ancient beings had many different skills. Some were great healers like your genetic line, while others were skilled in various sciences, and some were royalty since their expertise was the ability to inspire and lead people. Therefore, the fear is not strong in my genes like it is for the townspeople. I know the Gatekeeper is a myth created to keep the people enslaved. The royal blood of truth still runs through me and allows me to see things as they are and not as I am told they are. It is why I risk my life to bring the sick to you. I know you understand, because you risk your life to save them. I believe we both have an agreement on a soul level to help save humanity from the atrocities the Priest and his ancestors have committed for many generations."

I thought about what she said. Did I have an agreement on a soul level? If so, did I have an obligation to marry Lusha? Or did I have an obligation to myself and my own happiness?

Gwenneth snapped me out of my mental ramblings when she said, "Christina is waking up now. Please Janna, go to her so she is not afraid. She does not know us and will be confused about where she is."

Gwenneth went to the hearth to heat some water for tea. I followed her and sat down at the table.

"What will happen to us if the Priest discovers we helped his granddaughter?" I asked. "What if Alyssia tells her husband?"

I worried about the possible outcome. We had never helped anyone in the Priest's family. He performed all his own healing rituals. Gwenneth and I understood how difficult it was to heal someone you love. You cannot be emotionally attached. In order to access healing energy you must be able to raise your own frequency into a state of complete, detached, unconditional love, love so complete you must be able to honor the soul's request, even if it is to let the physical body die. So sometimes we are successful and sometimes we aren't.

I could hear Janna tenderly talking to Christina. "You're better, my dear. The color is back in your face. How do you feel?"

"Tired," Christina said in her sweet little voice. "Where am I?"

"You are in a safe place. Go back to sleep and I will take you home soon. Your mother will be happy to see you are well."

"I love you, Auntie," I heard Christina say.

"I love you more than you know, little one. You are a joy in my life. I could never let anything happen to you."

The loving words between them gave me pause. I could feel my heart soften. Janna must think of Christina as the little girl she was never able to have. Christina was fortunate to have Janna as her aunt. Janna was a powerful woman. Anyone would think twice before going up against her.

CHAPTER EIGHT

THREE TIMES A WEEK I went down to our cellar to study from the sacred books of knowledge. On those days I did the sacred breath work at least twice. It kept the energy flowing into my brain, so I could think clearly and unemotionally.

Around noon one day I sat on a cushion in the cellar and prepared myself to begin. It had been a week since Gwenneth brought up the idea of marrying me to Lusha. I had to be prepared to discuss this the next time she brought it up. I knew her well enough to understand she wouldn't drop the subject. I could try to avoid her as much as possible, but eventually I would have to deal with her. I still felt resentful, so I decided to do something to clear my head with breath work. I don't want my decision to be purely emotional, as such decisions usually end in disaster. I thought about what Janna said when she talked about having an agreement on a soul level to help save humanity from the Priest's wrath. Did I have an agreement on a soul level to marry Lusha?

I crossed my legs, got comfortable, and silently asked to be filled with God's love, and for clarity to fill my mind. I did the breath work until I could feel my mind floating. I brought the same questions to the front of my mind while I was in this state and waited for the answers to come. I waited, and waited, but nothing came to me. Finally I gave up in frustration, got up and went outside.

"Jumper!" I called, and waited for him to come running. When he didn't appear I called him again. I assumed he was most likely exploring the woods, so I decided to walk to the lake and enjoy my favorite place. As I walked to the trees that marked the path, I thought of my life and was filled with joy. I realized how fortunate I was to have my freedom, and the ability to practice any sacred discipline I chose. My sister and I were sovereign. We made our own way in this world.

I thought of the townspeople, the worshippers. What a horrible life to live if you were a woman! A townswoman had no freedom except what the man in her life allowed. She was either controlled by her father or her husband, and was at their mercy for even the smallest infraction of the rules they set.

If I married Lusha, would I have to give up my freedom? Would he then have control over me? Are the men of the sacred work any different from the worshippers? Fear rose in me as I asked myself these questions.

The lake offered a beautiful view of the mountain. The sky was crystal clear. I sat down and drank in the view, took a deep breath and said, "My beloved God, thank you for my life. I am fortunate to have a different understanding than others. Those who are vengeful and petty in their thinking, may assume you are, too. Give them the wisdom to know you directly and experience your love, so they can know your truth. Release them from their fear and release me from mine. I humbly ask you to guide me in serving humanity, so one day all humans can experience the freedom of your love." I bowed in reverence. The answer had come to me. I got up to tell Gwenneth my decision.

I arrived home just before dinnertime, but could not find Gwenneth. I thought perhaps she had gone for a walk. Dinner had not been started so I decided to make a beef stew. I went to the cellar to get some salted beef and root vegetables. Beef was for special occasions. Tonight would be one of those. I had made an important decision and wanted to celebrate it with my sister who had given up her youth to raise me.

Biscuits would go well with the stew, and a pie would put the perfect touch to the meal. We had sour dough for the one, and containers of preserved fruits for the other. Soon the sweet aroma of the pie filled the air, and as I slid the biscuits into the hearth oven to bake, I heard the front door open. I turned to greet Gwenneth.

"Good evening, Sister, you are in time for a lovely dinner. I have beef stew simmering in the pot on the hearth, biscuits are baking, and there will be pie for dessert!"

"What is going on? I'm the one who usually makes dinner. I've not been gone that long. Did you think I wasn't coming back?" she asked with a laugh.

"Of course not, I know you will always come back, but I suppose there is always a first time, isn't there?" I laughed back. "Come, Sister, have some tea."

There are certain teas we drink frequently. One of them is dandelion tea. Dandelion tea is an old remedy said to be the cure for all diseases. I don't know about its curative powers, but it tasted good, and we enjoyed drinking it.

"What is this all about?" Gwenneth asked suspiciously.

"What do you mean, Sister?"

"I mean, Shriya, you don't usually cook meals."

"But I do bake, and since I was already baking sourdough biscuits and a fruit pie, I threw in a beef stew for good measure." I could tell she didn't believe me, but she was kind enough not to ask any more questions.

I served our meal, and we ate in good spirits. When we were almost through, I brought up how my day had been. "Gwenneth, I went to my special place at the lake today after my breath work. I know how fortunate I am, and how it compares to the lives of the town's women. It was as if I could feel their discontent and pain. All women should be able to have the same type of freedom I do, rather than be controlled by their fathers and husbands. Our father died when mother was still carrying me in her womb, so I have never known a father. You are unmarried, so I have never known a brother-in-law. If I were to marry Lusha, who is a man of the sacred work, will it be the same as marrying a worshipper? Will I be under his control, or will it be different because he recognizes we are all divine and filled with the glory of God?"

"That is a very good, very wise question, and I am sure you have given it a lot of thought. Let me see if I can answer you. Lusha is a man of the world but is studying the sacred work. Anyone who studies this work sees all people as equals. He would never try to control you or take away your freedom. However, you must also realize any decision you make after a marriage will also affect him. So you would necessarily include him in your decision making, as he should include you in his."

I thought long and hard about her words before I spoke, "Well," I said, "I have been doing a lot of thinking today. My desire is to help women, and I do believe on some level I have agreed to help women reclaim their power. One way I could achieve it is by doing the sacred work myself, which would not only change me, but add to the consciousness of the whole. My work affects the energy field, even if only in a small way. It makes a difference."

Gwenneth interrupted me. "It makes more of a difference than you probably realize. All thinking affects the group's consciousness, which strongly affects the energy field. Sometimes it can take many years for a single idea to change the consciousness of the group. You see, the worshippers already have a group consciousness…that is, certain beliefs they all agree on. If someone has a different idea it is usually rejected by the group. It doesn't matter how good the idea is or how right. Sometimes it is rejected with so much vehemence, the person with the new idea may be persecuted. Any group consciousness is alive with its own energy which affects the energy field."

"Can you give me an example?"

"Well, think about Janna," Gwenneth continued. "She lives in town with the townspeople. But she is not a worshipper. However, she is a prominent member of society, the wife of the market owner and financially well off. The townspeople depend on the market to survive. Therefore, she is respected by many. She attends their worship services as a cover so she is accepted by the worshippers. But she also brings the sick and wounded to us. Most of the worshipping men and a lot of the women believe only the Priest can heal. They have been told he is the only one authorized by God to do this work. However, Janna realized his healing abilities were very limited when her mother was sick.

At that time Janna took her mother to the Priest for healing. The Priest was unable to help her, but instead of admitting it, he proclaimed she was fine and sent her home. Janna knew her mother was still very ill, but she took her mother home and put her to bed as the Priest instructed. That very night her mother died. It made Janna realize the Priest might not be the spokesperson for God after all. Nevertheless, the group consciousness in town accepted that he was. So it became Janna's mission to change the group consciousness by bringing the sick to us. It's not that we are the only ones who can heal or are special. Anyone can learn to heal if he wants to. It is like learning to play the violin. Anyone can learn how to play, but some people have a natural ability, so it comes easier to them. It is the same with the healing arts. We have a natural ability, so it's easier for us."

"You say when Janna allows us to heal the townspeople, her goal is to change the group consciousness. How does that work?"

"Every time Janna brings a woman to us, it changes the way that woman thinks. It makes her doubt if what the Priest says is true. Most of the people Janna brings are women who have already seen the Priest and are still sick."

Gwenneth continued, "The women in our family have all been healers. There was a time when none of the worshippers would come to us for help because the risk was too great. Many of them died. That now even a small number come marks a tremendous leap in their evolution. My point is… Janna is changing thinking one woman at a time. The women must be secretive in order to survive, but they are now questioning what they have been taught to believe. Each time a woman questions the authority of the Priest, it affects the group consciousness and the vast energy field it involves. Eventually the entire consciousness will change. It usually takes about a generation for it to happen. But it starts with one person. Does what I have told you help you to understand?"

"Yes, but it doesn't really change my thinking. The second thing I could do to empower women is to give the gift of life. For that it is not necessary I marry. I could conceive without being married and continue our genetic line." I saw the look of horror on my sister's face. It was not acceptable to have a child out of wedlock. But by who's rules?

"Shriya, to bring a child out of wedlock would be to condemn the child before it even had a chance."

"Condemned by whom? The Priest? We don't believe in the Priest, so what does it matter?"

"It matters because the Priest believes a child conceived out of wedlock is the spawn of evil, the work of the Gatekeeper. The child and his mother both might be killed. You must not even think of such a thing!"

"That makes no sense. Since we do not honor the Priest's beliefs, he would never know if I were married or not. Our marriage ceremonies are not even recognized by the Priest, so what difference does it make?"

"Even though we have our own ceremonies, we honor the marriage accepted by the laws of the land. In order to have a child and not risk the chance of the child being killed, we are married in the worshipper's tradition...by the Priest."

I was in shock. "What!"

"You heard me. To do anything else would be to jeopardize the child's life. A life is too precious to take lightly. We do not risk the wrath of the Priest. Sometimes we must obey the current laws even though we do not believe in them."

"Nonsense!" I was becoming frustrated and could feel my anger rise. "With everything we know, we still pretend to go along with them? Doesn't this give them the idea we accept their beliefs?"

Gwenneth thought about what I said before responding. "Yes, to some degree it does. But it is the only way to ensure the safety and continuation of our family line, and the best way until the group consciousness changes. If there were another way, we would do it. It isn't simply about conceiving a child, it is about conceiving one with the proper bloodline. It is the only way to help humanity realize the divine lives within them."

Those last words stung. She had made it clear it was the bloodline that mattered. If I didn't conceive with Lusha, who could I have a child with? What other man would be acceptable to my sister? My exposure to men was limited. Was I really free?

I could feel my stubbornness assert itself. "Gwenneth, I have great concerns about leaving you. If I am going to do this, it has to be on my own terms." I took a deep breath and continued, "I'm willing to marry Lusha assuming he is in agreement." Gwenneth nodded with a tentative smile on her face as I continued with my demands, "I am not willing to move to his village. If Lusha wants to marry me and continue the bloodline of the sacred work, he must be willing to live here with us." I waited for her response. I could see she was taken aback by my requirements.

"Shriya, your terms are most unusual. You know it is customary for the woman to move to the husband's village. I do not know if your request can be granted."

"Well," I said," if it isn't, I will not marry him. It's that simple."

I was not going to back down. My decision had been made earlier at the lake. Nothing she could say to me would change my mind. I was willing to fulfill my destiny, but it would be on my own terms.

"Your sixteenth birthday will be next month. I will take it up with Jabbar when they arrive for your celebration. That is the best I can do."

CHAPTER NINE

I WOKE EARLY ON MY SIXTEENTH birthday, possibly the day of my engagement to Lusha. Well, it depends. I wasn't willing to give up my home. Lusha would have to make the sacrifice. I was giving up enough in agreeing to marry him. I liked my freedom and would not be unhappy if he refused to meet my conditions.

I thought about the significance of the day. In the eyes of the world around me, I would no longer be considered a child. From today I was a young woman, eligible to be married in a few years. If I was not married by the age of eighteen, I would be considered a spinster like my sister. I was not in love with Lusha nor had the faintest yearning to be with him even though he was a handsome man and came from a good family. I wondered if he saw me as a desirable woman. Of course, all the older adults would see us as a suitable match. Lusha was a nice person and would be a good husband. As long as he didn't try to tell me what to do, we'd get along fine. I would agree to mate with him, but only for the sake of having a child. I certainly wouldn't go through something like that unless I had to. I had seen farm animals mate many times and couldn't imagine what was enjoyable about it. But for the sake of continuing the family line and the sacred work, I would do it.

On a beautiful spring morning I called for Jumper, and we walked together to the lake where I bathed in the cold, refreshing water. We don't bathe much during the winter because the lake freezes over. We do heat water over the hearth fire, and wash ourselves with a wet cloth during the cold season, but there isn't anything like immersing yourself in the water completely.

Lusha and Jabbar were to arrive later today. I hadn't seen Lusha since his sixteenth birthday. I thought about the first time I met him on my thirteenth birthday, and how odd I thought it was when Jabbar said they had been planning the trip to our home for months. I even remember how he winked at Gwenneth when he said it. Jabbar and Gwenneth had been planning it for years. I wondered if Lusha knew. I'd have to ask him, and look directly into his eyes to see if he was telling the truth. I needed to know what type of man Gwenneth was trying to coerce me to marry. Would he start out the marriage with deceit or would he be honest?

Jumper joined me in the water. I used the herbal soap I brought to wash his fur coat. He'd smell fresh for a while. He seemed to have an aversion to any aroma other than filth. I knew it wouldn't take him long to roll into something dead, or the dung of an animal. But maybe we could get through the day with him smelling good for a change. I washed my hair and scrubbed my body clean. I swam for a while enjoying the weightlessness of my body as I floated on my back and looked up into the sky.

By the time Jumper and I walked back to the house I was chilled to the bone. I went in and settled into a chair by the fire to dry my hair. We had two comfortable chairs, one on each side of the fireplace, where we could sit at night and read. The mantel of the fireplace was lined with candles. We used them not only as a source of light, but for the atmosphere they provided. I could get lost in thought looking into the flame of a candle. But what I enjoyed even more was to stare into the flames of a roaring fire. I would go into a trance, and my mind would travel. I'm not sure where it went, but it took me deep into a state of contemplation. Whenever I was disturbed about something, I would focus on the flames. Many times an answer to a current problem would pop into my mind as I allowed a trance state to take place. This always brought peace and comfort to me.

I was surprised Gwenneth wasn't awake yet. I expected her to be up and about, fixing breakfast. I needed something warm to drink so I put some water on for tea. Even though I was sitting in front of the fire, I felt chilly and unable to warm up. I was just pouring myself a cup of herbal tea when Gwenneth walked toward me.

"Happy birthday, Shriya," she said cheerily.

"Thank you. I was wondering when you were going to get up."

"I've been awake for a while. I was lying there reminiscing about the sixteen years of your life. It seems only yesterday you were a little girl and I was kissing your scraped knees and lacing up your boots for you. You started your journey into womanhood three years ago, and now you've grown into such a beautiful young woman. I am so proud of you. Mother would be proud of you, too."

I looked at her in surprise. She very seldom mentioned our mother.

"Thank you, Sister. It means so much that you feel Mother would be proud of me. Thank you for the beautiful compliment."

"It is well deserved, Shriya. You are basically a happy person, and a joy to be around. You think things through before making decisions. You are dedicated to the sacred work. You love deeply, and when others are around you, they feel it. Lusha will be very happy to have you as a wife. You deserve only happiness and it is my wish that Lusha will bring even more joy into your life."

I felt humbled by the sincerity of her words. I walked over, put my arms around her and held her tight. "Thank you, Gwenneth, for everything you've done for me."

"It has been my pleasure and joy to raise you, Shriya. Now you are a young woman almost old enough to be married. It is hard for me to believe this day is actually here."

"Hard for you to believe?" I laughed nervously "Imagine how I feel."

Gwenneth laughed with me. "You will be fine. I have a birthday gift for you. Wait here; I would like to give it to you before anyone else arrives."

She went off and soon returned with a square wooden box about the height and length of my forearm. She set it down proudly on the table. "Come and see what it is."

I wondered what it could be…a new dress? A pair of shoes? At the market I had seen a pair of boots I greatly admired, made of supple black leather. They were shiny, laced half way up the calf, and had a two inch heel. Boots for young girls had only a half inch heel, and laced over the ankle.

My boots were old and had been handed down to me from Gwenneth. The boots I wanted were expensive and were made for women. Since I was becoming a woman today, I hoped I might receive them as my birthday present.

I opened the lid of the box. The box was filled with a rich purple cloth which I excitedly pulled back to reveal a crystal ball. I lifted it out carefully and held it up to a shaft of sunlight coming through the window. The suns rays through the ball created a reflected rainbow on the wall. I looked at Gwenneth in awe. She smiled at me and said, "Do you like it?"

"Yes, I love it!" I exclaimed. "I never thought I would have my own crystal ball."

"Well, I believe it is time you looked into the future yourself. You did it once when you were a child. Do you remember seeing the neighbor coming to our house before he actually did? You were at your favorite place and saw it in the lake."

"Yes, I remember. But I never thought I would receive anything as beautiful as this."

Gwenneth looked pleased. "I decided you deserved one of your very own. A crystal ball aligns with your frequency. When you gaze into it, you can see what is coming your way. If you are not happy with the picture, you have the opportunity to change it by using the power of intention with your breath work. Your intent affects the energy field. And the energy field contains an enormous amount of power, so the power grid holds all potential. The energy appears like waves. But when you put your intent into this field, the energy waves collapse into matter. So we are continually creating the matter around us, either consciously or unconsciously. Our brain is an antenna with the ability to pick up all thoughts, and we tend to create things unconsciously. It takes a lot of work to be able to monitor which thoughts we want to embrace and which we allow to pass through, so we tend to create things which are not always beneficial for us. It is actually easier to see into the future and change the future than it is to consciously monitor your thoughts all day long. It takes a lifetime of work to master your thinking. But you will have a lot of fun with this ball. I certainly enjoy looking into mine. As you know, I have used mine to change both of our lives."

"Dear Sister, I thank you from the bottom of my heart." I was so grateful my heart felt about to burst with love.

"You may want to put it away before any company arrives."

"Yes, of course, Gwenneth, thank you again." I put the ball back in its box, and placed it in the rear of the wardrobe chest. Then I returned to the fireplace and brushed my hair until it dried, reflecting all the while on what the day would be like. It would be different than my thirteenth birthday. The only company would be Lusha and Jabbar, giving me a better chance to talk with Lusha and ask him some questions.

Breakfast was placed on the table, but I was too nervous to eat much of it, and merely picked at my food. Gwenneth noticed and tried to reassure me. "Shriya, do not worry. Everything will be fine. I will talk to Jabbar about your request. If you were to leave, and live with Lusha, I would be alone here and would find it difficult to do everything by myself. I think Jabbar may understand it is reasonable for Lusha to come and live with us. We could use a man around here. The extra help would be wonderful."

She was right. The help would be appreciated. That cheered me up. I felt happier as I got dressed. I didn't have a new dress to wear, but I did have one that had been Gwenneth's when she was engaged to Jabbar. It was a satiny cotton, and floor length. Our everyday dresses were ankle length, as they needed to be practical for working. A dress that dragged on the ground got dirty quickly. So a full length dress was special. This one was light green with a jade stone sewn right in the center of the bodice. As I looked myself over I could see that the top of my breasts showed. I tried to pull the dress up but it had been designed to be revealing. I guessed it was because it was an engagement dress and not a birthday dress, and would provide a bit of temptation to the fiancé. The thought crossed my mind that Gwenneth had loaned it to me with the idea of enticing Lusha. Did he require enticing? I had been so consumed with what I wanted, it never occurred to me he might be as anxious. Maybe he didn't want to be married, either, and felt pushed into this as I did. Well, I would find out soon enough.

I usually kept my hair pulled back from my face to keep it out of the way, but today I let it hang down free. I tucked a jeweled comb in my hair. It had been my mother's. Her mother gave it to her on her wedding day. It had originally been given as a gift to my grandmother for a healing she performed. The comb featured a white sapphire set in white gold. A quick look in the hand mirror assured me the effect was stunning against my dark hair. I put on my old boots. They didn't look very good, but they would have to do.

I went into the living area where the fire was dying out. The sun was shining in our windows, warming up our home. We wouldn't build another fire now until the sun started to set later this evening. By that time, the day would almost be behind me. I took a deep breath and wondered how I would feel this evening. Would I be happy? Sad? Still anxious? At peace? Only time would tell.

"Gwenneth," I called "Where are you?" No answer. I looked out the window and saw her greet the Adani men. It was an opportunity to observe Lusha without his knowing it. His smile was heartwarming and came easily to him. After the three performed the customary bows, Lusha hugged my sister and held her tight. A few words were exchanged. Then, arm in arm Gwenneth walked between the two men towards the house.

Lusha was carrying a large wooden box. I guessed it was a birthday present for me. I was relieved the box was bulky. A box for a ring would have been smaller.

I hesitated about what to do. Should I wait to greet the men when they entered the house, or go outside to meet them? I decided to be brave, and walked outside.

"Hello, Lusha, Hello, Jabbar," I said. "Welcome to our home. Please come in." I stood beside the door and gestured them inside. Gwenneth entered first, Lusha and Jabbar followed. I closed the door and turned to face them. Lusha and Jabbar bowed towards me honoring the divine in me. I returned the bow, honoring their divinity. Lusha came up and hugged me. He whispered in my ear, "You look beautiful, Shriya." He pulled away, looked into my eyes and smiled his sweet smile. I smiled back and felt my nervousness leave me. Jabbar came over and hugged me, too. The thought came to me he could be my father-in-law. I had no experience of a father. My life could change a lot this day.

Gwenneth took Jabbar's cloak and motioned for him to sit down in one of the chairs. She looked at me and said, "Why don't you and Lusha go for a walk. You have much to talk about."

I couldn't believe she did that. Was there to be no small talk? I suppose it was better just to get on with it.

"Alright," I replied "Let me get my wrap." It was still a little chilly outside. I grabbed my wrap, Lusha opened the door and I walked outside with him right behind me.

"We have a bench on the other side of the house," I said. "We can sit there and talk."

"That sounds like a good idea to me," he replied.

Wordlessly we walked over to it. Lusha took off his cloak and spread it over the bench. "The bench will be cold. This will help you stay warm," he said.

I sat down on his cloak and turned to look at him. "Happy birthday, Shriya," he said. "This is for you." He held out the wooden box.

I thanked him and placed the box in my lap. When I lifted the lid, I gasped. There were the beautiful boots I admired at the market.

"Oh! How did you know?" I immediately pulled them out of the box and put them on. I stood up and admired them. I bent over and hugged Lusha as he said, "A little bird told me. I am happy you like them."

He took both of my hands as I sat back down and said, "Shriya, I will be very honored if you decide to be my wife. I have had the opportunity to observe you the few times we've been together. Even when you were thirteen I could see you were a sweet, smart girl with a respect for all of life. You are dedicated to the sacred work and you are a great healer. I think we would make a good match. I am a member of the Sacred Knights, a secret order, and have studied their work all my life. I promise I will honor and respect you as my wife if you so choose."

"Lusha, you are a dear, sweet man. But I cannot leave my sister alone here. She has no one else but me. Our only surviving relative is our mother's sister, Aunt Kalini, who is several days travel from here and not allowed in these parts by order of the Priest. I have told my sister the only way I will agree to marry you is if you are willing to move here and live with Gwenneth and me." I said it, without waiting for Gwenneth to discuss it with Jabbar. This was my life and I would take control of it.

Lusha nodded. "To be honest with you, that crossed my mind, too. I wouldn't want to see Gwenneth alone. I had this discussion with my father. He's decided Gwenneth could come live with us if she likes."

I was stunned by his response. Considering past circumstances, it seemed more than a little strange to have Gwenneth move in with Jabbar. "It's hard to believe that at one time your father and my sister were going to be married."

"What?" he asked as if he didn't hear me.

"Some time before Jabbar married your mother, he and Gwenneth were betrothed, and very much in love."

"Then why did they not marry?"

"I thought you knew."

"No, and I ask you again, why didn't they marry?"

"That part of the story is not mine to tell. I only bring it up because it is ludicrous to think my sister would be willing to live with you and Jabbar when he already has a wife. It would be a cruel thing to do to her." I became angry. Did Jabbar think he could have my sister as his mistress because his wife was bedridden? Gwenneth would never stoop so low.

"This is the first I have heard of them ever being in love, so I am at a loss for words, I will need to discuss it with my father. Please forgive me if I have said anything to offend you."

His politeness was getting on my nerves. I would have rather had him pick a fight with me over what I told him than to be so apologetic. It would have been easier to argue about, and I was looking for any excuse to get out of my decision. Why did he have to be so nice? The reality hit me: I was going to have to go through with this. I had agreed to get married; not to Parkin, but to Lusha. My future included an arranged marriage.

I must have looked sad because Lusha asked, "Shriya, are you alright? Are you cold? You look concerned. I think we should go inside now."

"Yes," I said, hoping I did not sound too forlorn. "If you are in agreement, please talk to your father about you living here with us."

"Of course, Shriya, of course." He took my hand and I felt a small shiver run through me as we walked back to the house.

CHAPTER TEN

As soon as Gwenneth and I were alone, I asked her about the conversation she had with Jabbar. She was a bit evasive, not eager to answer me. I found it suspicious.

"Please tell me," I pleaded. "Did he say he wanted you and me both to come and live with them?"

"Shriya, don't be silly. That would be ridiculous."

"I called it ludicrous when Lusha proposed the idea to me. I think Jabbar may want you to be his mistress since his wife is bedridden."

"Shriya, watch your tongue! Don't make accusations which have no basis in fact."

"I am not accusing anyone falsely. Lusha told me it was Jabbar's idea. And Lusha didn't know you and Jabbar had once been betrothed. He was shocked when I told him."

"You told him about Jabbar and me?"

Suddenly I understood their betrothal may have been a secret. I felt slightly ashamed for not considering Gwenneth's privacy. I had been too consumed with my own feelings to think of hers. I said meekly, "Was I not supposed to? I didn't know I was to keep it to myself. I never mentioned why the marriage didn't take place. And when I realized he didn't know, I said no more. Please forgive me, Sister."

Gwenneth sighed. "Never mind. I know you meant no harm. If Jabbar wants to, he will tell Lusha the details. It will help his son understand why it is important for you two to marry. It is a great responsibility but an honor to be chosen."

I didn't see it, but I decided to keep my mouth shut. However, I wasn't going to let her avoid my earlier question. "What did you and Jabbar talk about?" I asked again.

"I didn't bring up anything important. It was too soon. I hoped we could simply relax and enjoy a casual conversation. There will be plenty of time for the serious discussions."

"Plenty of time? How long do they plan on staying?"

"Oh, I don't know. I suppose as long as it takes to agree on all the arrangements."

Fear hit me. Would Lusha never leave? Would I be expected to leave with them? No, I wouldn't do it! But I wasn't ready for him to stay, either. I had expected Lusha to go back to his home with Jabbar. Only later would he move in with us. I needed time to adjust to the idea. I needed time to say goodbye to the life I was living now. I could feel myself start to panic. It must have shown on my face because Gwenneth asked me, "Are you alright? You don't look so good. You've gone pale, and the light around your body is closing in around you."

Sometimes I hated her ability to see such things. It was hard to keep anything a secret. Her inner sight came in handy when we worked on healing others, but it was annoying when she used it on me.

"They must leave, Gwenneth. They must leave and give me time to adjust to becoming a wife." I could feel a sense of urgency as I continued, "I 'm not ready to give up being alone with you right now. You must make that part of the agreement. They must leave and come back at a later time, next year or the year after, when I am eighteen."

"They will leave when the negotiations are complete. Lusha's return, as well as your wedding day, will be part of the negotiations,'

I could hear the words, "*your wedding day*" echo in my head. I got sick at the thought of it. A wedding day meant a wedding night. I turned and walked away. Gwenneth called me back, but I ignored her. I went outside and strode toward the barn where I could escape prying eyes. I sat on a bundle of hay and thought about future sleeping arrangements. To provide us with at least a minimum of personal privacy, Gwenneth and I slept in separate beds, each of us in our own small areas of the house. Soon there would be another person sharing my space and my bed. It was hard to imagine. Maybe after we were married, I could convince Lusha to sleep in the barn. Why not? I had always enjoyed it.

This birthday was not turning out well. Instead of being a celebration of my sixteenth birthday, it had become a celebration of my betrothal, one that hadn't even been agreed upon yet! And all because my sister's life got messed up years ago. Now I was made to feel guilty when I simply wanted to live my own life and choose my own husband.

I wanted Parkin, and needed to find out if he felt the same way. If he did, I could run away. I plotted how to sneak away to see him. I would have to wait until Jabbar and Lusha left. I filled in some of the details, and when I was happy with my plan, I returned to the house, finally ready to relax and enjoy my birthday celebration.

Chapter Eleven

WE CELEBRATED MY BIRTHDAY THE next night. In spite of all the emotional tension of the proposed marriage arrangements, we had fun. We laughed, we sang, and best of all we danced around the bonfire. It was a beautiful, clear night. The moon shone brightly and lit up the sky. We could see the stars and other planets shining down upon us to remind us we were never alone.

Gwenneth and Jabbar finally decided Lusha would live with us. He would come late summer or early fall of the following year when I was seventeen. But first he needed to help harvest the fields at home where the two men grew corn, wheat, barley and several kinds of beans. The delay was good news for me. It would give me plenty of time to make arrangements to be with Parkin. If there was any hope we could be together, I needed to know it, and as soon as possible. I couldn't marry Lusha without knowing how Parkin felt about me.

I worried if I was attractive enough for Parkin. I knew I was smart enough. I was highly educated, Gwenneth had seen to that. She had also made it clear we were "different" than the townsfolk, so I understood why I didn't fit in. She believed in living a humble life, and I can honestly say we managed to do that well.

In order to see Parkin, I would have to be careful. Almost daily, Gwenneth would look into the future to see what time lines had been created specifically for me. But she was so caught up in the business of my upcoming marriage, I knew I had at least today, and maybe tomorrow, before she would start to peer into her crystal ball again. Jabbar and Lusha were leaving right after breakfast the next day, so my trip into town would have to be tonight, under the cover of darkness. I would spend the better part of my day in focus. I would focus on traveling safely and seeing Parkin, or at least be able to leave a note for him on his boat. But what if neither he nor the boat were there? Suddenly I remembered my sixteenth birthday present from Gwenneth… my crystal ball.

I had been so consumed with the marriage negotiations I had quite forgotten my new tool for seeing into the future. I smiled to myself. Gwenneth wouldn't be the only one who was able to see what was coming and change it.

I got up and dressed quickly. Lusha and I had become friends during his time here, so I felt guilty about what I was about to do to him. If everything worked out as I planned, I would break our marriage pact. He didn't deserve it, but I didn't deserve to be made unhappy either. He would learn it was for the best. I imagined him finding the love of his life and being grateful I had relieved him of the burden of marrying me. I was sure time would show I had made the right decision. Lusha's short term hurt would eventually give him long term happiness.

Lusha and Jabbar both embraced me before they left. It was apparent they were satisfied with the negotiations. Lusha didn't seem to mind he was giving up his life to come and live with my sister and me. Gwenneth was elated, too, almost prancing around in her glee. I will probably never understand her. I was happy to see both men go. We waved goodbye until they were out of sight.

Gwenneth immediately busied herself outdoors, while I entered the house and retrieved the wooden box that held my crystal ball. I could hardly wait to see what it would show me. I set the ball on the table, lit a candle and sat directly across from it, focusing on the flame in an effort to still my mind. Then I turned my gaze into the crystal ball while allowing my mind to go into a trance. But I saw nothing, no matter how hard I concentrated.

Eventually I gave up in frustration. It occurred to me the technique of working with the ball might be similar to the technique of working with the focus wand. I had practiced and practiced with the wand and never achieved any real success. I decided I would go to the cellar to practice the sacred breaths, and then I would attempt it again. The sacred breath was effective in allowing my mind to soar into other dimensions. It caused my body to vibrate at a higher frequency, and uplift me.

When I was finished with my breathing exercise, I did my best to stay in that state of consciousness, walking slowly and deliberately back upstairs to where the ball rested on the table. Fortunately, Gwenneth was still away. I settled in front of the ball and concentrated on my two targets, the town and Parkin. At first I didn't' see anything, but soon a mist formed in front of my eyes, similar to the one I saw at the lake so many years ago. As I continued to stare, the mist cleared, and I saw Parkin. I had to calm down my reaction at seeing him. By putting my emotions aside I could stay clear and see more.

As I watched the scene unfold, I saw Parkin climb off his boat and walk towards town. On the street he encountered a beautiful woman. She was large breasted and her tight dress showed off her hour glass figure. I wondered who she was and if he was attracted to her. Was she one of the ale house girls I had heard about? My emotions took over, and the scene disappeared. All at once I was choked by intense jealousy. I hated the woman, yet I didn't know who she was. My reaction surprised me. I realized I was no longer in focus. My emotion had taken me out of the trance.

I contemplated the vision I had seen. Now, more than ever, it was essential to find Parkin. I needed to tell him how I felt, and I needed to find out if he felt the same way.

I planned to leave after nightfall. The only thing that would ruin my plan was if Gwenneth decided to look into the future. I didn't think she would, at least not tonight.

Gwenneth had been bouncing with joy all day. She had finally accomplished the task she set herself to before I was even thirteen. I wondered what would happen to her if I ran off with Parkin. She would be left alone to care for our small parcel of the land. Would she be able to manage? She was a strong woman and could do it, I knew, but she would be crushed I had not lived up to her expectations.

After dinner, I retired early saying I was exhausted from the excitement. When I said goodnight to her, she responded in a curious way, "Always be careful of what you see. Things are not always as they seem." I had no idea what she was talking about.

I lay awake for what seemed like forever, listening for Gwenneth to go to bed for the night, and eventually she did. I waited until I thought she was deeply asleep. Then I slowly got up, my heart beating fast with anxiety. I had gone to bed dressed so I would be ready when the time came to leave. I put on my old boots and tiptoed out the door to the barn where I had locked Jumper in one of the stalls, so he couldn't go galloping about in the woods. I wanted him to accompany me on this journey. I could tell he knew something was up by his eager greeting.

We went down the road towards town, Jumper always slightly ahead, but within my sight. There was a full moon so I could see around me to some degree. I marveled at the midnight sky. Nature never ceased to amaze me. The stars were brilliant and the moon glorious in its fullness. I even saw what I believed to be fairies out of the corner of my eye. At first I ignored them, but after a while, their continual movement became annoying. I stopped and looked directly towards the woods. There were fairies everywhere! I stopped on the spot and stood gazing at them. Some were playing, some chasing each other, some basking in the light of the moon. It amazed me I could see them so clearly. But I had an important mission to carry out. Reluctantly, I continued on. I would have liked to tell Gwenneth what I had seen, but how could I explain my walk in the middle of the night?

As I continued, I imagined what it would be like to walk hand in hand with Parkin along this road. I wondered if he would be able to see the fairies, and hoped so. But what I hoped most was that he would want me as much as I wanted him. I understood why I was so drawn to him. It was because of the short life we had together in the past. Something about him made me feel safe. I knew he would protect me and take care of me, and I would do the same for him. Lost in thought, I soon arrived at the edge of town.

I called Jumper and commanded him to stay by my side. I needed his protection, and in any case did not want him running around to alarm the townsfolk who were not accustomed to encountering a wolf on the streets. As I walked through town, I was surprised so many people were out and about. I had expected most of the town to be asleep. But I wasn't going to back down now. I had come too far, and I also knew I might never get another chance

I pushed through the town and made my way toward the dock. My original plan was to check first for Parkin's boat. If it was there, I would knock on one of the windows. As I got closer, I strained my eyes to look for it. And there it was, docked by itself in all its glory! My heart leaped. He was there. Now I had to find him. I walked up to the boat to get a better view. I looked for any candle flames or burning oil lamps which would give an indication if someone was aboard. It appeared dark and empty. Jumper and I turned around and walked back to the main street. There was a lot of commotion in the ale house area. Parkin might be there. If he was, it would pose a problem since women were not allowed inside. Well, some women were, but I was not one of them. Parkin would soon see he didn't need a girl like that around him. He needed me. I would love him and educate him. It didn't matter he hadn't been born into the genetic line Gwenneth honored. I would honor him by teaching him sacred knowledge. I assumed he would have the desire to learn.

I stood outside the ale house, jostled by passersby, and wondering what to do. Everything else looked closed except the Inn where lights still shone from burning oil lamps. Maybe it was still open. I decided to make my way there. It would be nice to get out of the chilly air and contemplate my next move. As I walked down the middle of the street trying to avoid the crowds and the gutter filth, I saw two people walking arm in arm. They were very involved in their flirtation and didn't notice they were headed right towards me. I heard the woman giggle at something the man said. I assumed she must be one of the ale house girls; no self-respecting women would be so silly and flirtatious in public. I started to move to the right, so they could pass. As they got closer, my heart almost stopped beating. It was Parkin.

"Parkin?" I said.

He turned my way and looked quizzically at me, "Shriya?"

I smiled. I was so happy to see him, and waited a moment for him to ask the woman to leave.

"What are you doing here?" he asked with deep concern.

"I came to see you."

"Is something wrong? Is it Gwenneth?" He looked down at Jumper by my side.

"This is Jumper, my pet wolf, he won't harm you."

Parkin seemed uncomfortable, but pressed me once more. "You haven't answered my question. Why are you here so late at night and alone?"

Instead of answering I looked over at the woman, and then back to him as if to silently say, "Please send this silly woman on her way so we can talk privately."

He quickly said, "Please forgive me. Shriya, this is Vanita, my betrothed. Vanita, this is Shriya. She and her sister Gwenneth live on the outskirts of town."

I could feel myself go pale, "Your betrothed?" I asked in shock.

"Yes, we were betrothed last week. Is everything alright with you?" he asked again.

"Uh, um," I stammered. I didn't know what to say. "Yes," I mumbled, not too convincingly, and lowered my eyes to the ground. "Everything is fine. I must be going. Please excuse me."

Painful as it was, I forced myself to lift my head, and walk away. I kept walking as if I had a purpose for being in town. I held my head high as my sister had taught me while white hot pain seared my heart. Tears stung my eyes, and the more I tried to hold them back, the more they stung. When I reached the edge of town I burst into a dead run down the road. I ran and ran as fast as I could. Jumper ran alongside of me whimpering as he went. He knew something was wrong. Soon the tears blinded me and I had to stop. Jumper came up and licked my face. He nuzzled into my shoulder as he tried to sit in my lap. I hugged him and held him tight. The warmth of his furry body felt comforting on this chilly night.

I was deeply embarrassed. For years I had assumed Parkin loved me, or at least hoped he did. It was hard to believe I had dreamed about him all this time for nothing. How could I have been so wrong? Obviously, he didn't love me. He was in love with a ale house girl. What a wretched thought.

I stood up and resigned myself to marrying Lusha. At least Gwenneth would be happy. If I was lucky, I would be able to sneak back into the house, and she would never know what I had done. Her world would be intact. But mine was now destroyed.

Jumper and I slowly walked the rest of the way home. Sadness consumed me. I wanted to keep walking until I could walk into a different reality. I didn't want this to be my life anymore. My life of freedom was about to end. The life I had fantasized about with Parkin would never be.

When we got home I thought about putting Jumper back in the barn, but decided at least one of us should be able to live a life of freedom. So I let him roam the night as he saw fit. I opened the front door slowly and crept my way to my bed, changed into my bed clothes and settled in. I let out a heavy sigh. At least I had accomplished leaving and entering the house undetected. I could be grateful for that, or so I thought.

CHAPTER TWELVE

THE NEXT YEAR WENT BY much faster than I would have liked. Before I knew it winter was coming to an end and spring was revealing itself on the horizon. I wasn't sure when Lusha and Jabbar would be arriving, probably in a few short weeks. Their arrival had been delayed due to severe weather.

Gwenneth had been busy getting ready, and this day she was busy giving orders to me. "Re-stack the wood pile so it looks neater. Pull the weeds out of the flower beds and garden. Clean out the stalls in the barn." She had an entire list of what we needed to do to get ready for the wedding. And we weren't even getting married at the house, but at the worshippers' building. We would come home for the reception. I daydreamed about spitting in the Priest's eye during the ceremony. I hated that man. I hated him for disempowering women; for teaching of a vengeful God. As I saw it, he was ultimately responsible for my fate. Because of him I was destined to marry someone I didn't love. If it weren't for those of us keeping the truth alive for future generations, the people would be doomed to ignorance. I had finally come to terms with the idea that Lusha and I must marry to keep the genetic lines pure so the sacred work could go on.

I spent the day doing everything my sister wanted. We had to go into town so I could try on the wedding dress the seamstress made. Gwenneth and I had chosen a simple white cotton. We picked out a style fitted tightly around the bodice and waist, flaring out slightly below, and tied in back with ribbons. It was to be full length and would cover my birthday boots. I was excited about the dress. I had never had anything so lovely before. Nor had we ever allowed ourselves white clothing. It wasn't practical with the work we did. Most of our dresses were gray, black, and sometimes brown.

We woke up the next day and headed for town without eating breakfast… Gwenneth's idea. But I didn't complain; I was doing my best to stay on her good side and not looking for conflict. She was the rock in my life, the only person I had. We didn't say much to each other as we walked to town. I was lost in thought, and assumed she was, as well. On arrival I could smell the strong odor of fish coming from the docks. It instantly got me thinking of Parkin. I decided to push him out of my mind; I didn't need to think of him anymore. I forced myself to feel happy by recalling how nice Lusha was. He would treat me well. It would be a happy life, and Gwenneth was thrilled. I owed her this much, I reasoned. She had devoted her life to take care of me. I could at least make her happy by fulfilling her dream. The work would go on.

"Shriya," said Gwenneth, "I have a surprise for you."

I looked at her with anticipation, "A surprise?"

"Yes, we are going to the Inn for breakfast," she said proudly.

"We are eating at the Inn?" I asked in surprise.

She took my hand, and we walked quickly. I was indeed surprised as we had never eaten there. Before we walked in I stopped and whispered to her, "Sister, can we afford this?"

"I've been saving money in the flour jar for a special occasion. What could be more special than you getting married?" she asked.

I felt my heart grow warm. "Thank you," I responded humbly.

We went inside and sat down at a table. I noticed heads turn as we walked in. No doubt the townsfolk were surprised to see us. Most of our visits were to the market, and then we would hurry away. I felt somewhat intimidated but remembered what Gwenneth had always taught me, "Hold your head high. You are no greater or less than they. We have all been created equal. That is God's law." Gwenneth was wise. I was proud to be her sister, but still uncomfortable sitting inside the Inn.

The inn keeper came and offered us some ale, and explained what was available to eat at that hour. We declined the ale, saying herb tea was our drink. I decided to have Roasted Tenderloin of Beef. Gwenneth had the same. It was served with parsnips, an egg and a pile of boiled carrots. The beef was the tastiest, most tender I had ever eaten. As I enjoyed my food, I became more relaxed. Gwenneth talked on and on about how nice it was going to be to have a man around the house. I had to agree; another person would ease the work load for both of us.

Gwenneth soon excused herself to use the outhouse behind the building. I was apprehensive at being left alone. She assured me I'd be fine during the short time she was gone.

"Alright," I said quietly, "but hurry."

As she got up from the table, I felt everyone in the room look our way. I put my head down and tried to avoid looking at anyone. I pushed the food around on my plate trying to pass the time until she returned. I heard the door open but avoided looking up knowing it was too soon for it to be Gwenneth. Then I heard my name spoken by a voice I recognized. I raised my head, and standing in front of me was… Parkin.

"I keep seeing you in places where I don't expect you to be. Are you alone?" he said.

"No. Gwenneth stepped out for a few minutes."

"Then I'll be quick." He pulled a chair out and sat down next to me. I felt uncomfortable about the last time we had seen each other. I didn't know where to look so I focused on his mouth instead of his eyes.

"I want to tell you," he continued, "I have always admired you and hoped to get to know you better. There is something special about you. But your sister made it clear she did not want me to talk to you. She warned me that if I pursued you in any way she would cause me problems."

I felt my face get red and I wasn't sure if it was from the anger I felt for Gwenneth at that moment, or the embarrassment I was experiencing because of her past behavior.

"I, uh, I am so sorry," I stammered.

"I thought you should know the truth. It's not that I haven't been attracted to you. Quite the opposite. I've dreamed about you for months. I dreamed about a life we had together before incarnating into this lifetime. We were deeply in love then. But my life was taken early, so it was a love we never really got to fulfill. But I haven't forgotten. I've been looking for you my entire life. I only became betrothed to Vanita because I knew your sister would never allow us to be together."

"But an ale house girl, Parkin?"

"What are you talking about? Vanita is not an ale house girl. She is the granddaughter of the island's chief scribe. She and her mother moved there after her father died of influenza. Is she the reason you ran off so suddenly when we last met?"

"Yes. I was shocked to hear you were to be married. It didn't really matter to whom. But I am relieved to hear she is not one of the girls there is so much rowdy talk about."

"You should know me better than that," Parkin chided.

"But that's the problem; I don't know you as you are in this life."

"And your sister will never allow it."

My heart sank. So many thoughts raced through my mind I had trouble finding a response.

"Shriya? What are you doing?" Gwenneth come rushing up to us. "You are not to speak to this man." She turned to Parkin. "I told you to leave her alone," she said in a harsh whisper. She grabbed my arm and took me outside.

"Stay here and don't go anywhere," she said sternly. She went back inside.

So it was true. She had warned Parkin to keep away from me. My head swam. I thought about what Parkin had just revealed to me: he also remembered a previous life we had together! My dreams of that life explained the immediate connection I felt with him. His must have had the same effect. I wondered if we would have to go through still another lifetime without being together.

I was lost in thought as a young man of slender build with short blonde hair approached me.

"Excuse me," he said, "Can you spare a coin?"

"Uh, no, I don't have any coins." I answered hesitantly. I expected him to keep walking, but instead he stopped and engaged in a conversation with me.

"It's a beautiful day isn't it?" He stated it as a mere matter of fact more than he was actually asking me. When I looked at him to respond, I noticed how blue his eyes were, they seemed to sparkle.

"Yes, it is. Are you new to the area?" I said. Instead of answering my question, he started talking about the sky; how the clouds reminded him of patches of snow. I continued to stare into his eyes as I wondered who he truly was. Just then, Gwenneth came out of the Inn and walked past me. I expected her to be upset that I was talking with another man. I think she expected me to follow her, but I found that I couldn't move. I just stood there staring as she walked away from me. Then I turned to look back at the man with the blue eyes. He was gone. I looked down the street. I didn't seem him anywhere. I looked all around, and he was nowhere to be seen. I continued to stand there transfixed with confusion on where the man had disappeared to. When Gwenneth realized I wasn't following her, she stopped, turned around and walked back to me.

She stood in front of me, grim faced, arms on hips. "Well, Shriya," she demanded, "What did Parkin say to you?"

"Did you see him?" I asked with anticipation.

"Of course, I saw Parkin. Why do you think I went back in there?"

"No, not Parkin, the other man I was talking to when you came out."

"There wasn't any man talking to you when I came out," she said with exasperation.

"Yes, there was. There was a man with crystal clear, deep blue eyes."

Gwenneth ignored me. I realized she was not hearing what I said, nor was she interested. It dawned on me that maybe I was the only one that had seen him. I was quickly snapped out of this contemplation as Gwenneth continued to question me. "What did Parkin say to you?"

"Nothing, Sister, nothing important. He was just making small talk. That's all, just small talk." I didn't see any reason to discuss it with her. She wasn't going to let anyone or anything stop her from achieving her dream of seeing me marry Lusha.

We walked to where the seamstress lived. She had a room dedicated for sewing. On its shelves were neat piles of material from homespun cottons to the finest of silks. I went through the motions of trying on my wedding dress, still numb from hearing what Parkin had said to me. As I glanced down at myself, I couldn't help but admire how beautiful the dress was. It was gathered at the bust under a wide, square neckline. The long, fitted sleeves were puffed at the top. The skirt flared out gracefully and came down to the floor. I spun around and watched the skirt twirl. Yes, the dress was beautiful, but not enough to quiet the anxiety which came over me when I realized the full impact of what I was about to do. I was going to live my life to please my sister, and wed a man I didn't love. At this point there seemed to be no other choice. My wedding day was drawing near, and Parkin was engaged to marry another woman.

At the market we bought some fish to cook for dinner, and left for our long walk home. Gwenneth could tell something was wrong by my silence, so she kept talking about things she thought would cheer me up. Meanwhile, I tried to put the conversation with Parkin out of my mind. I would wait until I was alone to think about what had transpired today, fearing if I confronted Gwenneth with it I would lose my temper and say things I couldn't take back. So I kept my silence.

CHAPTER THIRTEEN

I NEVER DID TELL GWENNETH ABOUT the conversation I had with Parkin. I didn't see the point. She believed she was doing the right thing. Nothing I could say would change her perception. Anyway, I had decided she was right. I was destined to continue the sacred work. With that in mind, I decided I had better make a serious effort to learn. If I couldn't have true love in my life, I should at least be able to master the focus wand. So I kept up my practice and got better at it every day.

I carried my wand to my special place, and after sitting and thinking for a while, I decided to commit to the practice of rearranging matter. I needed something to practice with, and looked around to see what I could find. A rock? No, I wanted to use something more alive. I saw an old pine cone on the ground, reached down, picked it up, and turned it over in my hand, but that didn't seem to be the right object either. Nearby, a wild cherry tree was beginning to bloom. "That's it," I thought. I would use one of the cherry flower buds which would be bursting with spring energy, and ready to make a change. I walked over to the tree and broke off a small twig that had a single flower bud and brought it back to where I had been sitting. I placed the twig on top of a boulder located several feet in front of me. With my wand on my lap, I decided to focus on the twig first.

As I looked at it, I went into a trance and allowed myself to go deep... deep... until I began to feel myself melt into the twig, then I pointed my wand towards the branch. I closed my eyes, concentrated my mind into a single stream of consciousness and allowed the passion for this work to come into my body. I no longer saw the cherry bud in my mind. I saw a full blown pink flower with a ripe red cherry hanging from the branch. I held the image until I couldn't hold it any longer. My mind started to wander, so I opened my eyes and discovered the sun had started to set. I must have been in focus for over an hour. The cherry bud and twig lay unchanged on the boulder. "Even so," I told myself, "at least my focus ability has improved." I decided I wouldn't give up. I wasn't willing to let frustration, disappointment, or any other emotion get in my way.

It was time to go back to the house. The animals needed their evening feed, and I was sure Gwenneth would be preparing dinner by now. When I walked in, she looked up and expressed surprise when she saw the wand in my hand.

"I don't know what I was thinking when I gave up so easily," I told her. "I wish I had stayed with it. Who knows what I would be able to do by now?"

Gwenneth looked at me compassionately. "Shriya, I am happy you have changed your mind and are willing to pick up the art of transmutation again. If you remember, you used to believe it would not serve you."

"Well, Sister," I replied, "I cannot think of a situation in which I would ever need to transmute matter from one thing into something else. But, for some odd reason, I am very compelled to practice this."

"Sometimes we don't understand why we are drawn to do certain things, but the future eventually shows us. You are old enough now to listen to your heart and intuition and follow it without question."

When I awoke the next day, I was filled with determination. I felt I could conquer the world as I walked to my special place. I held the wand directly at the twig. I closed my eyes and felt the power surge in me. Passion exploded out of my heart center. I was determined to turn this twig into a gold coin, so instead of seeing a twig, I visualized a shimmering gold coin before me. I held the focus and felt the energy. At first the image was a mixture of hazy pink and gold colors, then the pink slowly faded and only the gold was left. It shone with such a bright light I thought to close my eyes, until I realized they were already shut. I felt something shift within me and heard a slight thump. I opened my eyes, and there sat a gold coin. I bent over slowly to pick it up. I turned it over in my hand. I had done it! I had successfully transmuted matter. I sat there stunned and shaky, relishing my accomplishment.

I closed my eyes and thanked my beloved God for the miracle I had just performed. I would be fine. I was now able to accept I was part of the sacred work. I was ready to live out my fate.

Chapter Fourteen

Before I knew it, my wedding day arrived. Lusha and his father were already here. They had bedded down in the barn the previous night to allow the bride-to-be a sound sleep. I secretly suspected they were afraid I would change my mind and run away, and were doing everything they could to keep me happy. But happy I would never be as long as I could not be with Parkin. I would be content to marry Lusha, but I didn't see how I would ever be really happy. Aunt Kalini was coming for the wedding day. We expected her earlier, but apparently she had been delayed. I looked forward to seeing her again. I never did get a chance to question her about my mother. But this time I was going to make it my mission to get some answers.

Aunt Kalini arrived shortly after breakfast. I saw her coming, camouflaged as a man. I jumped up and ran outside to greet her. "Aunt!" I yelled as I ran to her and embraced her with a big bear hug. She wrapped her arms around me and held me tight. Her fake beard tickled my face as she kissed my cheek.

"Shriya, how you've grown! You have become a young woman in the past few years."

"Yes, faster than I would like," I replied. "Come Aunt, come and eat. We still have some breakfast left."

"I am famished," she admitted. "And I would love to have some food. I had expected to arrive last evening, but on my journey here I came across a little boy who had the flu. I performed a healing on him, and stayed with his parents for a while. They were afraid he would not survive. But he woke up this morning feeling wonderful. I slipped out right after."

I understood. If townsfolk found out you had the power to heal, it could put you in jeopardy. So it was probably best she departed before the word spread.

I sat with Aunt Kalini as she ate. We finally had time to speak together privately, as Gwenneth had gone for a walk with the Adani men.

"As you know," I began, "my sister is not willing to talk about our mother very much, and I have many questions. Will you allow me to ask them of you?"

"Yes, dear. I will do my best to answer them. But understand, the conversation must stay between the two of us."

"I will keep whatever you tell me to myself," I assured her.

"Alright then, go ahead."

"My first question is, how did my mother die?"

My aunt leaned in close to me as she answered. "She was burned at the stake for being a witch."

I gasped. "For healing the sick?"

"No. It is a long story, but if you are interested I will tell you what I know."

"Please, I want to know everything. I am tired of all the secrecy."

"Has your sister ever told you why she never married?"

"Yes, she said she was attacked by a young man and hurt so she could never bear children. She also told me that prior to the attack she was betrothed to Jabbar, Lusha's father. That's why it is so important to her that I marry Lusha. It continues her plan of carrying on the blood line."

"Right. But there is much more to the story." Aunt Kalini paused and looked down at the table. She pushed aside a few crumbs of bread. "Shriya, this story has been kept from you for a reason. You needed to be older to understand and accept what happened." She looked directly into my eyes as she continued. "The young man who hurt your sister was the Priest's son, Devon."

"How can that be? Devon is a married man now, with his own children. Why isn't he locked up in the tower or hanged for such a violent act? Surely any man who would hurt another would be punished," I said.

Aunt Kalini went on. "When Gwenneth told your mother what happened, you mother went straight to the Priest and demanded something be done to prevent Devon from ever hurting another woman. The Priest refused to do anything. "Gwenneth has only herself to blame," he said. "She must have seduced my son into such an evil act. Possibly she is a witch, possessed by the Gatekeeper's evil.""

"How could he blame such an awful thing on her?"

"It isn't uncommon for a woman who has been raped to be blamed and burned as a witch. The Priest teaches if a man is tempted to take a woman in that manner, she must be under the Gatekeeper's spell. Devon wasn't much different than his father, although they revealed their evil in different ways. But evil is evil. When the Priest blamed Gwenneth for Devon's behavior, it was more than your mother could bear. As she watched her daughter bleed for days and witnessed the pain she was suffering from a brutal rape, hate began to consume her."

"What did she do?" I asked apprehensively.

"She took the matter into her own hands. Your mother learned that a servant in the Priest's household was a young girl Devon had also raped. Devon got her the job to keep her quiet and available. The girl had no family and nowhere else to go, and she feared if she did not accept the work she would be denounced as a witch. She agreed to the arrangement, and was still living and working as a servant for them. Your mother was able to obtain her cooperation easily, and together they devised a plan to slowly poison Devon. They didn't want him to die quickly. They wanted him to suffer."

"And suffer he did. He became seriously ill. His hair started falling out, and he grew very pale and weak. Eventually he became bedridden. This went on for weeks. Their plan would have worked, but they let him linger too long before giving him the fatal dose. As it turned out, the girl was finding it difficult to get access to his food, and asked one of the cooks for help. This cook had been like a mother to her, and hated Devon. But the Priest had become suspicious, and questioned the cook. He threatened to have her stoned if he discovered she was responsible for what he assumed was his son's food poisoning. Her job was to purchase all the foodstuffs and make sure they were properly cooked. The Priest had no inkling the poisoning was deliberate. The cook became afraid for her life and told on the maid servant. But despite the cook's pleading innocent, she was taken away and later stoned to death."

"The servant girl was questioned, too, about where she had obtained the poison herb. She understood she was doomed either way, so would not name the responsible party. But the Priest knew the ultimate guilt rested with the few people who still had the ancient knowledge of plants. It wasn't too hard for him to jump to the conclusion that person was either Gwenneth or your mother."

"Did the Priest kill my mother?" I asked in horror.

"Yes, my dear. He did. Now you know why it is so difficult for your sister to talk about her. She blames herself for your mother's death. Everything was taken away from Gwenneth in the span of a few months. She lost her betrothed and the life she was to begin with him. She lost her mother. She lost everyone but you. You are her reason for living. If it hadn't been for you, she would have probably died of grief. Caring for you gave her the will to go on."

"I'm surprised the Priest didn't have Gwenneth killed."

"He may have wanted to, but after your mother's mortal life was taken, I gathered up you and your sister and we went into hiding."

"You did?" I tried to think back to the time my mother suddenly disappeared. "I vaguely remember you coming over and waking us up in the middle of the night. But that is all I recall."

"You were only three years old. I'm surprised you remember that much. I took both of you away to the musician's house. Remember the two musicians who came to your thirteenth birthday?" I nodded. , "We stayed with them until things calmed down. After several weeks, we came back. All your family's livestock had been killed and left to rot. The Priest's soldiers stole what they could find. Fortunately they did not find everything. The cellar was left intact. So our wine and sacred objects and books were left untouched. But there was an extremely old vase that had been passed down our family line for many generations. It was beautiful, priceless, and irreplaceable. It ended up in the hands of the Priest."

"How did you know when it was safe to come back?" I asked her.

"You have been taught how to look into the future, but there is another technique you have not yet been told about. It is the ability to look into the past. You select your target the same as you do for the future. You focus on the day and person or place you want to see. But instead of a crystal ball, you use a mirror. The mirror shows you the past: who you've been, where you've been, past events, anything you want to know. I looked and saw what your mother did to the Priest after he murdered her."

"What do you mean" I asked.

"I knew your mother well. I knew she was not going to let him get away with killing her daughters. The Priest was mistaken in thinking that once he killed someone, the person was dead. The body may be gone, but the soul lives on in an essence no one can kill. We are made of energy, alive with or without a body. In some cases, not having a body actually makes it easier to influence this plane we exist in. Once we leave our bodies, we have a much wider vision of what is happening. We are not limited by the blinders we sometimes wear while inhabiting a physical body."

"I'm not following you, Aunt Kalini."

"I will tell you what I saw when I put myself in a trance all those years ago." She began the story. "Something told me to take a look at the Priest and see what his life was like since my sister's death. I put myself into a trance with both the Priest's and my sister's essence as my target. At once I saw him in his bedroom, asleep. Suddenly he sat upright. He must have heard something which startled and awakened him. As he peered around, a picture hanging on his wall fell to the ground, breaking in several places. I could see he was shaken, but he seemed to brush it off, and returned to bed. As he turned over to go back to sleep, a vase went flying off his chest of drawers. It, too, shattered as it crashed to the floor. He sat up and shouted. His mouth formed the words, 'Who's there?' He threw his bed covers to the side and started to get up, when the lamp in his room suddenly lit itself. The fear on his face increased."

"I knew he could excuse the picture falling down and the vase falling off the dresser, but he couldn't pretend an oil lamp could light itself. It was impossible. His hands trembled as he got up and went to the fallen picture, a portrait of his son, Devon. Looking at the shattered vase his strongmen had stolen, he became even more frightened. The words my sister spat at him before the fire took her life, undoubtedly rang in his ears, for he clasped his hands over them but was unable to quiet her voice in his head: '*Let my death be enough for you. If you even think of hurting my children in any way, I will haunt you. I will never leave you alone! You can kill my body, but I will continue to exist in the ether. You cannot touch me there, but I can touch you, and touch you I will if you ever plan to harm my girls.*'"

"Put into the ether, the power of those words created a force that has automatically protected you and your sister from the Priest. Your mother's words still protect you. But as you have grown older and more powerful, the force of them got weaker because you did not need as much protection."

"As for the Priest, the next morning he canceled the search for you and your sister. But to this day, I am not safe from his wrath. The Priest is afraid to harm either of you, but he does not fear me the same as he fears my dead sister."

Chapter Fifteen

It was a tradition for the wedding party to be escorted to the worshippers' building, and four of us climbed into the carriage the Priest had sent. Jabbar, Gwenneth, and I sat inside. Lusha sat on top with the driver. Aunt Kalini didn't want to risk the wrath of the Priest, so she stayed home to prepare for the celebration, and would be there to greet the musicians when they arrived.

It was a rough ride. I had never ridden in a carriage before so the time went by fast. The scenery looked different from this new perspective. The horses were beautiful creatures, but skittish, as if picking up on my nervousness. I had never been inside the worshippers' building where the townsfolk met regularly to hear about the evil of the Gatekeeper. I was worried about exposing myself to an atmosphere where fear was taught. Gwenneth sensed my uneasiness. She reached over and placed her hand on top of mine, whispering, "There is nothing to be afraid of. This is simply a formality. Remember, if you are not married by the Priest, he will not honor the marriage. And any child born of it will be considered a spawn of the underworld and killed."

The Priest scared me, but I knew I had to let my feelings go. I didn't want fear to be a controlling factor in my life. I had watched it destroy the common sense of the townspeople, who were so addled by fear they could no longer reason anything for themselves. At times, their actions were despicable, yet they behaved that way because the Priest told them to.

When we arrived, Lusha jumped down and helped me out of the carriage. He was always considerate, and I believed I would be content with him. It's what I told myself whenever I started to think about Parkin, because at last I was convinced I made the right decision.

Lusha and I walked through the front door arm in arm. The Priest was waiting for us. I noticed he didn't look at me, and barely glanced at Gwenneth, but kept his attention on Lusha and Jabbar. I didn't know if he avoided us because of the story my aunt told me about my mother haunting him, or if he disregarded women in general.

The Priest gave the men instructions on what was expected. I stood off to the side in my wedding dress, holding a small nosegay of seasonal wildflowers. Lusha, too, was in his wedding apparel, a tight-fitting green doublet over his best shirt, and black hose on his long slim legs. The doublet brought out the color of his green eyes, and emphasized his muscular build. I had to admit he looked very handsome.

The Priest motioned for Jabbar and Gwenneth to stand slightly to the side of us and for Lusha and me to come forward. Before I could move, my sister whispered in my ear, "I am very pleased with you. You have made our family proud."

I walked up and stood next to Lusha. His tall stature, muscular torso and straight bearing gave him a look of authority. The Priest was at least half a head shorter, and maybe because of that he didn't seem nearly as menacing as he had before. Lusha turned to me and smiled as if to say, "Come, come be my wife. I will honor and love you. I have enough love for both of us. Do not worry. We will have a happy life together."

I smiled back and directed my thoughts to him, "*It is not that I do not have love for you, it is that I am not in love with you. But I will make the best of this and be content with you.*" I knew he couldn't hear my thoughts, but it gave me comfort to send them anyway. Maybe someday I would have the courage to say them out loud. Or maybe I didn't need to. He probably knew them already.

The Priest started the service, but I was too involved in my own thoughts to pay full attention until he abruptly asked, "Who gives away this young woman?"

Gwenneth rose, stepped over to me and announced, "I do. Her elder sister. I give this woman to this man to be cared for, for all of her life." I noticed she didn't mention anything about love, or about me caring for him. Yet I understood I was being passed off from one caretaker to another.

The Priest continued on, but I wasn't really listening until I heard something about obeying. What did he mean by *obey?* No man would ever tell me what to do, and if he did have the temerity to try, I would not obey. Since I had no respect for the Priest, I found the entire ceremony boring and ridiculous. But I was doing my duty. I was being married according to the laws of the time. Thankfully, the service was short, and I was relieved when it was over.

The seating arrangement changed on the way home. Jabbar and Gwenneth sat on top with the driver. Lusha and I had the carriage to ourselves. You cannot imagine how awkward I felt. I didn't know what to say to him. He tried to start a conversation several times, but I was reluctant to keep the talk going. So instead of fully responding, I spoke only a few words, and instead of admiring my new husband, I stared out the window to admire the view.

When we arrived home the musicians were already there. Aunt Kalini had trenchers of food set out everywhere. She and Gwenneth had been cooking and baking for several days, while I had been banned from kitchen duty all week. By the looks of things, you would think we were expecting an army; there was enough food to feed one. When I commented on the amount, Aunt Kalini grinned and said, "We are expecting a lot of company. This is an important day to many."

She was right. A great number of people came to celebrate our marriage, people I had never met. I didn't know it before, but many of them were hoping for this marriage. Members of the Sacred Knights attended, as did men and women who had been studying the sacred work all their lives. One by one they came up to me and wished me well. They assured me my decision to continue the sacred work would be honored in ways I could not imagine. They were right. I couldn't begin to imagine it. But instead of saying so, I nodded and agreed with them. It was easier that way.

The celebration lasted well into the night. Eventually it was announced that my husband and I should be off to our marriage bed. This was something I was not looking forward to. Tired as I was, I did not want the evening to end. Gwenneth had discussed with me the necessity of performing this physical act to conceive a child. Since I had agreed to marry to continue on the blood line, I had no choice but to fulfill my obligation.

All too soon Lusha and I were in my sleeping space, newly sheltered with hanging fabric. I was nervous and didn't know what to do. I sat on the edge of the bed. Lusha came and sat next to me. He took my hand and said to me gently, "Shriya, we will not do anything you are uncomfortable with. I am happy to sleep on the floor if you like."

I reached out and touched his face. "Thank you," I said, "Thank you for allowing me the time to adjust to this new life. But you need not sleep on the floor. You are welcome to share my bed with me. However, I do request we each sleep on our own side. That will be enough of an adjustment for me right now."

I took my finger, and drew an imaginary line down the middle of my bed and said, "That's your side and this is mine." Lusha smiled. He wasn't going to give me any reason to dislike him. I found this extremely irritating. At the same time, I found it comforting. I could feel at ease with him. I didn't have to worry about him making demands on me.

We slept in the same bed on our wedding night. He stayed on his side, I stayed on mine. We slept way past sunrise. We even slept past breakfast. When I woke up, I found Lusha sitting up in bed watching me.

"What?" I asked.

"Nothing, I'm admiring your beauty."

"Are you making fun of me?"

"No, my dear," he reached over and brushed the hair out of my eyes. "You really are beautiful. I like watching you sleep. You look so peaceful."

I felt a slight rush of emotion when he pushed the hair away from my face. It was nice to have someone touch me. I knew Gwenneth loved me, but she seldom showed it in a physical way. I wasn't sure what the rush of emotion meant, but I decided I liked it.

As time went on I felt more and more comfortable with Lusha. We had moved on a bit in bed, to where he held me while I slept at night. During the day he was always kind, and went out of his way to please me. The simple things he did impressed me, and the fact he listened to me even when I rambled on about nothing. I found myself enjoying his company, and one day, when he went into town by himself, I actually missed him. I had grown accustomed to having him near. It was fun to have someone to talk to. Gwenneth didn't always like it when I talked too much; she found it annoying. But Lusha seemed genuinely interested in whatever I had to say. He was starting to grow on me.

I sat at the table outside watching him chop wood. He was handsome, strong and lean. The sight sent a rush of feeling over me. It was the same whenever he touched my face. Something about his touch caused a pleasant reaction in me. I made a decision I knew he would be happy with.

We went to bed early, both tired from a long day's work. He held me like he always did, but this time I slowly turned my body to greet his. I looked at his full, red lips and raised myself up slightly so my lips matched his. His head bent down towards me, and our lips met and locked together. The contact sent a vibrant shock through my body.

Any fear or anxiousness I had disappeared, and a wild feeling took over. I had never experienced sexual passion before. His hands found every curve of my body as we made love for the very first time.

Afterward, I lay in his arms exhausted yet exhilarated. I slept well in his embrace, comforted by the idea of him watching out for me. I would be safe and secure with him, my husband.

Not every night was so benign. I still dreamt about Parkin, and often those dreams were nightmares. It was the same dream over and over: Parkin falling overboard and me searching for him in the vast, unforgiving sea. I would wake up sobbing and screaming. It frightened Lusha half to death. I could never tell him what my nightmares were about. He knew I had them regularly, so he would comfort me by holding me, and stroking my hair until I fell back to sleep. He was a kind man.

CHAPTER SIXTEEN

WINTER CAME AND WENT AND spring was upon us once again. I celebrated my eighteenth birthday with no sign of pregnancy. Gwenneth was more disappointed than anyone else.

The winter had been busy with many sick women and children brought to us. Some felt awkward because there was a man in the house, but Lusha was adept at making himself scarce during those times. Since the visitors usually came at night, I think he was happy to stay in bed and sleep. We made it clear to him that healing was woman's work and he was not needed or wanted during those times.

Winters could be harsh. We always had a lot of snow, and with the cold weather came illness. Respiratory problems were common. Influenza ran rampant throughout the town. Every year a few of the worshipping men were lost to the flu. I wondered if they realized, once their spirit left their bodies, that their prejudice against women healers caused their death. I never mentioned this to Gwenneth or Lusha. They would have lectured me about cultivating a loftier view of men, and I didn't want to hear it. I wanted to think of them as being stupid people who gave away their power to the Priest, and not only denied their own inner power, but persecuted women who claimed theirs.

Since Lusha had arrived we acquired a few more pets. I hadn't known his love for animals when we first met. He was constantly setting live traps to see what small animals would turn up in them. We now had a wild, miniature pig. Lusha trained it like a dog. Jumper wasn't too happy about it, but eventually the two learned to tolerate each other. I could tell by the look in Jumpers eyes he would have preferred to have the pig for dinner, but Lusha kept it in an enclosed pen so Jumper wouldn't be too tempted.

One day when Gwenneth and I came home from the market we found we had inherited a snake. Gwenneth shuddered, but Lusha said the snake represented the powerful energy inside each of us, and was the symbol for the universal ether. "In your own ancient, sacred books there are drawings of serpents wrapped around the spine reaching into the brain," he declared. "Surely, Gwenneth, these show the significance of the snake."

"I know of no such thing!" Gwenneth retorted. "Now get rid of this creature. Wild animals belong outside, not indoors."

I couldn't help but laugh over their disagreements. After all, it was Gwenneth who pushed this marriage, and now she had to live with Lusha and his habits. She wasn't used to being challenged. She'd had her own way for so long, I think she forgot how to compromise.

Lusha won the battle of the snake. He built a small container for it and kept it near our bed. For the first two weeks I slept with one eye on the container. Lusha said it was only a garden snake and harmless. But I wasn't so sure. I would never understand his fascination with trapping animals, and why he thought he needed to take away their freedom. He insisted they loved being his pets, but I had my doubts.

Lusha had carved a new focus wand. He was supposed to deliver it to a young man who turned thirteen the past November, but the weather had made traveling too difficult. I could only imagine the young man's disappointment in having to wait so long for it. Now that the weather had cleared Lusha could make the delivery. I wanted to go with him, but he said it was too dangerous. It wasn't only the risk of running into stormy spring weather. Focus wands were illegal. The consequences of having one could result in severe punishment. The Priest called them magic wands and thought the wand itself held the power. But what could you expect from an ignorant man like him?

As my husband prepared for his trip, I knew I would miss him while he was gone. He was a help when I needed something heavy lifted, and a comfort when I wanted companionship. Lately I spent a lot more time talking with him than I spent doing my sacred disciplines. He was an easy distraction. At the end of each day, I would berate myself for not having used the hours necessary to master any discipline. I would promise myself to do better the next day, but when the next day came I would find myself distracted once more. With Lusha gone I would have no excuse for avoiding practice.

I seldom ever looked into the future. Maybe I was afraid of what I would see. Gwenneth was happy I had married, and was waiting for me to announce a pregnancy. She hinted she had seen it her crystal ball. I wasn't as concerned. I knew if I did conceive, it would change my life forever. I was still adjusting to being married. I didn't mind waiting to experience being a mother.

I was beginning to daydream about Parkin again, and would chastise myself, thinking it was unfair to Lusha, who deserved my loyalty. My nightmares about Parkin continued, too, reminding me I was destined to live a life without true love again. It seemed unfair. But life wasn't always fair, I knew.

On the morning Lusha was to leave on his trip, I woke up early to fix his breakfast. His destination was a good three day's walk away through some heavy woods. Wild animals were always a concern but Lusha had a way with them. The dangerous animals in our forest were used to us. By mutual understanding, they posed no threat to us, nor we them. But when we ventured outside our own forest, it was a different story. The animals living deep in the wild were not used to seeing humans on a regular basis, or in sharing their woods. Fortunately, Lusha could see and communicate with the small forest creatures. They seemed to sense he meant them no harm, looked out for him, and warned of any danger lurking ahead. Lusha told me many stories of his previous forest treks. The tales brought me comfort. I trusted no harm would come to him.

I saw Lusha off and headed straight for my special place. Although I was not consistent at practicing my sacred disciplines, I never missed my morning meditations. It was a time for me to be silent. I loved the time to myself, and being in this natural setting rejuvenated me. If I felt a little off when I woke up, I had only to make my way to my meditation area, and all would be made right in my world.

Jumper walked with me until I arrived at the entrance, then ran off to explore. When I reached the lake I sat down. I had my focus wand with me and was determined to practice. I looked up toward the horizon and allowed myself to go into a trance. I could see the energy field in the sky. It appeared as transparent grid lines which danced with the movement of life. Seeing it helped me understand that everything was made of the ether, and the energy field was a viable living thing.

Eventually I closed my eyes and allowed my mind to go into a deep state of consciousness. At first, brilliant lights danced by, but as I allowed myself to go deeper I saw a swirling, ultraviolet blue, and let myself bathe in this color until it filled my body and mind. I never quite understood the significance of this, but always felt mentally and physically better afterward.

I slowly opened my eyes, and there in front of me stood three eight-foot-tall beings. I was so startled I screamed and jumped up. I turned and started to run, but tripped and fell. When I looked back, they were gone. I looked all around. Nothing. I was afraid to move because I didn't know where they had gone. I sat there for a long time before I got up enough nerve to make my way home.

When I arrived, Gwenneth was sitting in her chair mending a seam on one of her work dresses. I must have been a sight, because when she looked up at me she said, "You look like you've seen a ghost. Are you alright?"

"I'm not sure what I saw. But I saw something." I told her about the experience. "These beings were each about eight feet tall, and I couldn't tell if they were male or female. They wore full length blue robes emblazoned with stars and moons that shimmered in the sunlight. The robes had sleeves that fell below their wrists."

Gwenneth listened attentively, and after a long pause said, "It seems you have had a visit from one of the star families. There are many populated planets besides this one. They are the stars we see at night. The star people usually watch us from afar. They are concerned about the welfare of the humans on this planet, but seldom interfere."

"I have read about them in the sacred books, but I never expected to encounter any of them," I said.

"For them to show themselves, they must have taken a special interest in you."

"Why would they have an interest in me?"

"Why not? You are a practitioner of the sacred work. You married a man of a secret order. They have a vested interest in seeing you achieve your goal."

"What goal?"

"To help humans overcome their ignorant ways. They want us to continue the work to help change the consciousness of the common people, the worshippers. You already know how important it is for the townspeople to realize their own divinity."

"I don't see how that can ever happen. They think what they have been told, and do not believe the ether is a universal energy. They discredit anything that empowers them with the mind of God."

"True, but we all can get overly emotional, and be fearful, too. Being a human brings that on. And it is why the ancient ones still watch over us. They listen to our prayers and intervene when we ask."

I was surprised and said so. "I didn't realize the ancient ones were still around. I thought it was up to us to continue the sacred work. If they are watching us why don't they appear and perform their miracles like they used to, and show the worshippers what they can do?"

"Their planet circles ours only once every three thousand six hundred years. They visit oftener than that, but it is not always easy or practical for them to do so. For short visits they must enter an energy vortex in the ether to transport them through time and space into another dimension."

I shook my head. "I'm confused," I admitted.

"For now, yes. But as your studies continue you will be taught how to accomplish such a task."

"I want to learn now," I said.

"All in good time, Sister, all in good time. You are not yet ready to work on such advanced conditions."

Disappointment settled in my stomach. "How much longer do I have to wait?"

"You may not ever learn to accomplish such a feat during this lifetime. However, it is said that when the student is ready, the teacher will appear." She clasped her lands in her lap, and smiled at me. It was Gwenneth's way of ending the discussion.

But I couldn't forget about this new possibility. I changed the subject and asked her, "Why would beings from another planet, our star family, as you call them, care about what happens to us if their planet is so far away?"

Gwenneth responded with a calmness I wasn't used to seeing in her. "They are acting strictly from a place of love. They are evolved in consciousness compared to humans. They live in a state of unconditional love. Their love allows us to make our mistakes and learn from them. But there are times when they will step in and help us when we are on a destructive path and don't realize it. At times, our own fears can prevent us from evolving."

"Do you think I am on a destructive path by letting fear hold me back?" I asked. "Is that why they came to me?"

"No, Shriya. I don't think that is the reason they appeared. Maybe it was to let you know you were not alone. I am sure they are pleased with your decision to marry Lusha. Our work is selfless and extremely important to the evolution of humanity."

"Well, they frightened me. It would have been nice to know about their visits before they came calling." I promised myself I would find out how to travel through these vortexes. I would look it up in the sacred books. I didn't care if my sister thought I was ready or not, I didn't need her help or permission. I was determined to experience time and space travel on my own.

CHAPTER SEVENTEEN

THERE WERE NO MORE VISITS from the star family. I spent as much time as possible searching for lessons on vortexes and time travel. I didn't find anything, but I wasn't going to give up easily. I would keep researching in the sacred books until I found what I was looking for.

The days went by quickly while Lusha was gone. Gwenneth and I went into town. It had been a while since just the two of us had gone somewhere. In fact, the last time was when we had breakfast at the Inn. Our current excursion brought back pleasant childhood memories. Gwenneth, who had a tendency to be distant, was even more so when Lusha was around. This trip was an opportunity to spend some fun time together. No lessons, no lectures, simply enjoying each other's company. We had a pleasant walk and talked of many things. She asked if I was happy with Lusha.

"He is a very nice man," I responded. "I have no problems being married to him."

"How is your ability to conceive coming along?" she asked.

I wasn't sure how to answer. What did she mean by such a question? My silence encouraged her to elaborate.

"It has been six months, and you are still not pregnant. Do I need to give you an herb to make your womb ready?"

"No, thank you. My womb is fine. I will conceive when the time is right and when a child is ready to enter this world."

"Time is of the essence, Shriya. You never know what can happen in the future. Are you making yourself open to him?"

"Are you really asking me that?" I demanded. "How dare you! Of course, I am making myself open to him; I have never refused his affections." I didn't think it necessary to explain how patient he had been with me in the beginning. It was none of her business.

"Don't be angry," she said in her most soothing voice. "I am only saying it is important that you do everything you can to conceive as soon as possible."

"What's the rush?" I asked. "What did you see? Is something going to happen to him? To me?"

"No, I have not seen anything happening to you."

I noticed she didn't mention if she saw something happening to Lusha. I didn't push the question because I didn't want to know the answer.

We walked the rest of the way in silence. Why did she have to bring up something so personal, and spoil our one enjoyable day? Why did everything have to be about the genetic line and carrying on the sacred work? I wanted to have a normal life. I was tired of trying to accomplish all the different techniques. I wasn't very adept at them, and I knew it. I did my best. I tried. What more could anyone ask of me? Well, Gwenneth could. She kept asking and asking. I had married Lusha for her. That should have been enough.

The closer we got to town, the more depressed I became. I needed to snap myself out of this mood and be at my best. The townspeople were always a challenge. They still whispered amongst themselves whenever we were around, especially now we had a man living at the house. I'm sure that gave them plenty to talk about.

I decided I would only allow myself to feel joy. I would not let Gwenneth bother me. I would put her words out of my mind. I felt my step lighten as I made the decision. I was going to be happy no matter what.

We went into the market and traded our eggs for supplies we needed. Janna hadn't brought us any women to heal for a while, which was good. It meant no one had taken ill. I often wondered if her husband knew she did that. I figured he must, and was an extraordinary man to allow it. He was obviously not a worshipper, although he went to the building every week and attended the service. But so did Janna.

I thought about what Gwenneth had taught me about an entity named Abigor. After the ancient celestial beings left Earth, people lived peacefully for several thousand years. Into this peaceful world Abigor arrived. He came from a different galaxy, flying out of a black thundercloud in a fiery chariot. The people had never seen such a thing; they were awestruck and ready to believe whatever Abigor told them. He demanded all people worship him as their god. If they didn't, he swore to send them to an underworld for all of eternity.

He empowered one of his worshippers to control and rule the masses, and see to it the people followed the laws he set forth. Abigor gave this worshipper the title of "Priest". If anyone broke the laws for any reason, the Priest had Abigor's permission to torture or kill them. Abigor told the Priest to father a son, and for every generation of sons to do likewise, so that control of the people could be passed down through the generations.

Because of this, the sacred teachings had to go underground. If anyone was caught healing, transmuting matter or seeing into the future, they were judged to be possessed, and were condemned. If anyone even hinted they had access to the universal energy field and could create and control their reality, it brought them immediate death. The plan worked well to control the mass of people, and still works to this day.

As Gwenneth was doing business with Janna, I excused myself. Gwenneth looked at me anxiously. I said I needed some fresh air, but the truth was I wanted to go to the docks and see if Parkin's boat was there. I wanted to see Parkin. I didn't know why. It made no sense. He was probably married by now, and I was definitely married. But the longing I felt for him could not be denied.

I walked to the docks with great anticipation. I looked, but his boat wasn't there. The disappointment was crushing. I had wanted so much to see him. He had probably settled down to domestic life by now and perhaps no longer went out on the boat. I walked back to the market and waited outside for Gwenneth. Sadness overcame me. I had missed my chance and would probably never see him again. I should have asked him not to marry

Vanita. I should have proclaimed my love to him. I should have, but I didn't. Gwenneth was right; I was destined for something else.

On our walk home I didn't bring up our previous conversation about becoming pregnant and neither did she. We kept our conversation superficial, talked about the garden; what we had planted and what we expected to happen with the weather this year. We had a pleasant time as we pulled our cart, loaded with our fresh supplies, behind us.

As soon as we got home, I went directly to the garden. Working in the garden always made me happy. I loved putting my hands in the soil. I became so engrossed in weeding I didn't hear my sister walk up.

"What in the world are you doing?" she questioned, "You haven't stopped for three hours."

I looked up, my hands covered in soil. A few hairs fell down into my face as I smiled at her. "I'm making room for joy in my life. If my life is created out of the ether from my state of mind, then my mind must be cluttered. Everywhere I look I see clutter, stuff overflowing in the house, and weeds overtaking the garden. Somewhere I lost my joy. I'm not sure where, but in order to restore it, I have to make room for it. So, as I clean out these weeds, I hold the vision of joy. I'm cleaning out all the past, all the guilt and self-pity. I'm ready to have joy again!" I declared with enthusiasm.

My sister looked at me, as she so often did, with the amused expression of an adult listening to a child. She never understood me or how my mind worked, and it led to a lonely life. She and I shared the same family line, the same sacred knowledge, but I still felt alone. I always had the feeling she thought I was too simple minded to understand the greater things in life.

Going into town made me realize how unhappy I had become. The disappointment I felt when I didn't get to see Parkin overwhelmed me. It was Parkin I loved, not Lusha, whom I had married. I did it to please Gwenneth, and it was a mistake, one I would have to live with for the rest of my life.

CHAPTER EIGHTEEN

Lusha had been gone for almost two weeks, and I was mentally preparing myself for his return. I was planting lettuce in the garden when I saw Janna walk up our road looking very determined as she strode towards the house. I couldn't remember Janna ever coming alone during the day, and reckoned there must be a problem. I got up, brushed the dirt off my dress, and headed for the house as I called out to her.

"Janna, what brings you out this time of day?"

She turned and came rushing towards me. "Shriya, I have very bad news. Lusha has been arrested."

"Arrested? For what?"

"He was arrested on his way to the village. One of the Priest's men followed him and stopped him. He was searched, and found with a magic wand. He was arrested on the spot and has been held in the village this entire time. The Priest had him transferred to the town's tower. I saw him being escorted there this afternoon. He looked fine, Shriya; he looked tired, but he looked fine."

I was horrified. What was I supposed to do? "Gwenneth!" I yelled, "Come quick. We have a serious problem." Gwenneth was already walking towards us.

"Lusha has been arrested. He was caught with a focus wand."

Gwenneth and I looked at each other. We didn't need to say anything. The expressions on both our faces said it all. We both knew the consequences of being caught with such a thing. The Priest was terrified of the wands, convinced they held great power. Wands had been outlawed for years. We had been able to keep the fact we even used them as a secret for several generations. There would be serious repercussions.

"I can talk with my husband," Janna said. "I can see if he is willing to speak with the Priest on Lusha's behalf." I appreciated the offer, but knew it would do no good. This was an offense the Priest would not take lightly. He behaved as if he had control of everyone, but would now be aware that secret goings-on were happening behind his back. It was terrifying to think of what might happen to Lusha and the rest of us as a result. The Priest left us alone as long as he thought we were harmless. If he knew we were practicing empowering techniques, our lives would be in jeopardy.

"Let's go in and talk," said Gwenneth. "We'll have some tea while we plan what to do."

Tea? "Gwenneth, tea does not make everything right," I said. "I can't drink tea when I am this upset. Lusha will most likely be killed, and you want to have tea?"

Gwenneth came over to me and put her arm around my waist as she guided me toward the house. Janna followed. I didn't say another word. What would happen to Lusha, what would happen to Gwenneth and me? This was very, very bad news.

We sat at the table, and Gwenneth questioned Janna about what happened.

"I only know he was arrested because he was caught with a magic wand," Janna said.

"It is not a magic wand. It is a focus wand." I was upset as I said it. But I was so tired of the ignorance of these people. I realized by the look on Janna's face that I had offended her. "The wand isn't magic," I said in a softer voice. "It is merely a tool used to help the untrained mind hold a focus into a single point of concentration."

"Well, that may be, Shriya," Janna responded, "but the Priest believes the wand is magic, and he is afraid of it. Telling him it is a tool to train the mind will not help your case or Lusha's. He probably fears the power of your mind more than the wand itself. Your best option is to minimize the power of the wand. You certainly don't want him to know you can transmute matter with the wand or your mind." She looked at me as if to say, "Do you understand?"

I was taken aback by her words. How did she know we used it to transmute matter? She must have figured out what I was thinking because she added, "I am aware of what the wand is used for. There was a time when some of our family practiced the arts. But that was a long time ago."

Aha! This explains why she brought the sick to us. Either she didn't have an interest in the arts herself, or she was afraid to practice them but was still able to contribute to healing in her own way.

Gwenneth addressed Janna directly, "You know the Priest better than either of us. How do you think we should proceed in getting Lusha released?"

"I don't know. Fear is the Priest's most effective tool to control others. We understand its power. It is hard to tell how far people will go when fear is their motivation."

"Can we turn the tables on the Priest and use fear to control him?" I asked.

Gwenneth answered, "We could, but the problem is, he has laws backing him up and a great many people who support him and his laws. There are ways to get around this, but then we have to ask ourselves if it is the ethical thing to do. If we use fear, are we not then the same as he? Would we not be lowering our own consciousness to his level? We need to ask ourselves, in the light of eternity, will we be happy with this decision? When we pass this plane, and we have our life review, will we be proud of this?"

Oh! My sister could be so annoying, so righteous. Couldn't we simply do something out of pure meanness because the Priest deserved it? Did we always have to be so pure and analytical? I wanted Lusha cleared. I wanted revenge on the Priest, and I said so. "The Priest has outlived his usefulness. Let us poison him and be done with it." I looked over at Gwenneth expecting her to be shocked by what I said.

"We can do that. But what will it get us? Almost the entire town supports him and his laws. If we get rid of him we will still have the whole town to deal with. Do you want to poison the entire town?"

"Well, maybe we should," I said. "We can put them out of their fear."

Now it was Janna who looked at me aghast. "Shriya you can't mean that! There are children and innocent people in the town. Many do not even support the Priest, but feel they have no choice but to pretend to. They may not be strong enough to stand up to him, but they do not deserve to die."

"No, of course not, I didn't really mean that," I said apologetically.

"Let's all calm down," said Gwenneth, "We are all on edge, and concerned about what to do. We should not allow our emotions to get the best of us."

I knew she was right, but I did want revenge on that man. I hated what he represented and secretly blamed him for my life. If it weren't for him and his ways I wouldn't have to live a secret life. I could practice the arts openly, and so could anyone who wanted to. I wouldn't have had to marry by arrangement to keep the bloodlines pure. If everyone were free, there would be no reason to have pure bloodlines. I understood this well, and wondered if Gwenneth did.

"I think I should speak with my husband," Janna said. "He and the Priest are good friends. Let us see what he can find out. I will return as soon as I know something."

Janna left. At first, Gwenneth and I did not talk. What could we say? Our lives were in danger. We were stunned and afraid, and didn't need to say it out loud. After a while, finding the silence oppressive, I said, "Gwenneth, do you think we should look into the crystal ball?"

"First we need to ask ourselves if we will have the ability to change the timeline if we see something we don't like. As you know, in order to change the outcome we must remain detached. If we react from emotion we will have no power to change it."

"That's true," I said, "But I feel so helpless."

"We may feel even more helpless if we are not able to alter what we see," she responded.

Tears stung my eyes. I didn't want to cry, but I couldn't stop the tears from coming. Soon they were streaming down my face. I put my hands over my face. How could this be happening? I was worried about Lusha. I was worried about Gwenneth, and yes, I was worried about myself. Everything

I lived my life for could be coming to an end... the end of the genetic line and the end of all of us.

Fear won. We did not use the crystal ball. But a powerful force would not let us remain in fear for long. What we tried to ignore came to us that night in our dreams.

I didn't sleep well; bad dreams kept me awake. I suspect Gwenneth didn't sleep well either. The next morning we didn't say much to each other, but occupied ourselves with chores to keep our minds busy. However, the nightmares I had all night long haunted me during the day. The image of Lusha slumped over in a corner, beaten and worn down, wouldn't leave me. I decided to tell Gwenneth about it.

She was in the yard, digging up an old stump. As I explained my dream to her, she looked upset and asked if the dream was in color.

"Yes," I replied. "The colors were very bright."

"I had the same dream," Gwenneth confided. "Mine, too, was in vivid color. It is a sign the dream is not a product of our own brain, but our mind dipping into the energy field where all things exist. We call this lucid dreaming, because we are seeing actual events which have already taken place. So Lusha has been beaten. It would not be uncommon, considering the situation."

She spoke as if it were a simple matter of fact. I, on the other hand, felt very emotional.

"We must heal him," I said in desperation. "We must do what we can to help. Please, Sister, let us start now."

At once, Gwenneth put down the shovel she was using; brushed her hands off on her skirt and went into the house. I followed. Gwenneth went to our altar and lit a candle. "We will do a distance healing," she said. She took out a quill pen, ink pot and a bit of paper on which she wrote Lusha's name, and under it drew a rough outline of his body. "We will both hold this as our focus," she instructed. "Our minds will enter the universal ether and change the energy pattern around Lusha's body. His flesh will transform itself to hold the new, healthy energy pattern."

Distance healing wasn't something we attempted very often. But this was an urgent case. It would be a challenge, but I knew we could do it.

We placed the drawing of Lusha on the wall directly behind the candle. I sat with my legs crossed and rested my eyes on the flame. When I felt myself drift into a trance, I closed my eyes and saw Lusha healed and perfect. I felt myself go deep into the far recesses of consciousness, as his image transformed into flickering lights. I was being drawn down a tunnel twisting and turning as the lights formed themselves into one large white light, then blue, then purple. As I continued to focus on the image of Lusha through the purple light; his body began to take on three dimensional form. I saw the purple wrap around him, the color radiating pure love and pulsing with life.

Suddenly the purple changed back to white. Then it broke up into tiny packets of flickering lights. After several minutes, I opened my eyes and continued to keep my eyes on the candle flame. I thanked God for the experience and for any healing given to Lusha. I stood up and bowed with humility. I understood God's love had flowed through me. It was important for me to set my personality aside and give the credit to God, as I was only a vessel for this powerful work.

Gwenneth was still looking into the candle's flame. I waited until she finished. I didn't speak to her about my experience. I was afraid if I talked about it, some of its power might be lost, and I didn't want to take that chance. Lusha's well-being was at stake.

We were silent for most of the day except for Gwenneth's singing. The mood had definitely lifted since our healing meditation. We didn't stop to think about the consequences of our actions. Lusha was hurt so we did what we do. We heal.

Later that afternoon Jabbar came to our house, visibly upset. He, too, understood the gravity of the situation. Gwenneth asked to speak with him alone, so I went outdoors. From the open window I could hear their muffled voices, talking excitedly as they outlined plans. I wasn't really paying much attention until I heard the word "bio-locating". I perked right up and went to the door. I pressed my ear against the crack between the door and the wall, hoping to hear more. I had heard of transporting a physical body from one place to another and wondered if the process involved vortexes.

"Before his marriage," I heard Jabbar say, "Lusha had practiced moving objects from one place to another with the power of his mind."

"How far had he gotten in the discipline of teleportation?" Gwenneth asked.

"The last time we spoke of it, he had mastered moving objects easily. But he told me he was only able to move his physical body short distances, but could not control the final location."

"I'm not surprised. That usually takes years of practice, and even then cannot be assured. We need to do something to help him now. But, what?"

"We must hold the idea it is possible for him to accomplish this."

Gwenneth sighed. "And if he is unable to transport his body, is there another way to escape?"

"The tower is heavily guarded. Escape is almost impossible. His only chance is to put all his intention and focus into bio-locating his body out of the tower. But he needs strength to do it."

I listened more intently. I now had more research to do in the sacred books about bio-locating and teleportation. I suspected these were somehow connected to time traveling. I was determined to find out.

"Shriya and I did a distant healing on him this morning. We both had vivid dreams he had been beaten. We wasted no time in giving him back his health and strength. He should be recovered well enough by the end of the day to practice bio-locating this evening."

"It would be best if he did it at night. That way, if he misses his mark and ends up somewhere he had not planned on, he will be hidden in the darkness," Jabbar reasoned.

"That's true," said Gwenneth. "Jabbar, you know Shriya has not progressed far enough in the arts to learn about this."

"I reckoned so," said Jabbar. "How is she advancing in the work?"

"Doing well. She doesn't always have the patience it takes to master something completely, so gives up too soon. Patience is a virtue she has not yet learned."

"Does it remind you of anyone?" Jabbar asked.

"No Jabbar. It does not." Gwenneth said. I had always seen that side of Gwenneth, but never seen it in myself. It was interesting to hear someone else's perspective of me.

CHAPTER NINETEEN

THE NEXT DAY, AFTER GWENNETH consulted her crystal ball, we prepared to go into town to see if we could talk with Lusha, although we hoped he had already bio-located himself out of there. Gwenneth's crystal ball had given no evidence of any personal danger we might encounter in town, but it did show my sister and me sitting by our fireplace this coming winter, and I was knitting something. I thought it odd, since I didn't know how to knit, but Gwenneth found it exciting. When I asked if she had seen anyone else with us, the answer was "No". It only meant we would be sitting safe and cozy next winter. It didn't mean anything bad was going to happen to Lusha.

When we arrived in town the whispers amongst the townspeople were worse than normal, so although I walked tall, I felt very small. Never before was it made so apparent how different we really were. It was one thing for the townsfolk to suspect what we did, but another to know for sure. The word had spread throughout the town that Lusha was arrested for having a wand on his possession. It meant we had been practicing the sacred arts and the sacred work they feared so much.

We hadn't been in contact with Janna since she informed us of Lusha's arrest, so we went to the market to see her. Janna was busy with a customer when we walked in. As soon as the customer saw us, she hurried out of the shop. Janna greeted each of us with a hug, and said, "My husband, Aapt, is in council right now with the Priest. He should be back shortly. Please help yourselves to a piece of fruit. It will sweeten your day." We all took one, although I didn't feel like eating anything sweet. Life didn't seem very sweet right now.

It wasn't long before Aapt arrived. His face went pale when he saw us. Jabbar spoke up, "Sir, please tell us what you know."

"I fear it is not good news," Aapt said. "When the guard went into Lusha's cell this morning, the cell was empty." A wave of relief came over me.

"The guard left to report his escape to the Priest, and found Lusha in the hallway. He was just standing there, and appeared to be disoriented. The guard easily apprehended him. However, the guard noticed Lusha's wounds had disappeared. It was a cause of considerable concern to everyone in the tower. Even the Priest began to fear the powers Lusha might have." Aapt looked down as he said, "Lusha has been sentenced to burn as a witch."

I gasped loudly as my hand flew up to cover my mouth. Jabbar began to shake, but said not a word. Gwenneth stared straight ahead and asked, "When will the burning take place? We need to know how much time we have."

"Today, at sundown," Aapt answered.

Gwenneth ushered the two of us out of the market and back into the street. "We must act quickly," she said. "We must see if we can visit him. We need to speak with him before....." Her voice trailed off without finishing her sentence.

"Speak with him about what?" Jabbar demanded.

"We must know everything he has told the Priest. Our lives could be in jeopardy, too."

Jabbar raised his voice, "Is that your concern? They are going to kill my son, and you talk of your own danger. Have you no shame?"

"Jabbar, lower your voice. We do not need anyone to hear us speak of such things. I am concerned not only about myself. I am concerned about protecting the knowledge. We must preserve the knowledge at all costs. You know that."

"No, I don't know that," Jabbar said. He turned away and strode off towards the Priest's building. Gwenneth quickly followed, leaving me standing there. I decided not to follow. This was a conversation I did not want to be a part of.

Gwenneth returned a few minutes later saying, "Jabbar is not thinking clearly. He is going to try to break Lusha out of the tower. It is impossible to do."

"How do you know it is impossible?" I asked.

"She looked at me sharply. "The tower is heavily guarded. Even if he can get in, he may not be able to get out. He is risking his own life. There are so few of us left, he should not be taking the risk. It is bad enough to lose Lusha; for Jabbar to risk losing his own life is unnecessary."

I could not believe my ears. I decided right then and there she had taken commitment to the sacred work too far. I would never again listen to her as I had in the past. How could she blame Jabbar in wanting to save his son's life? What father wouldn't? I decided not to respond to what she had said. What I had to say she wouldn't want to hear, nor would she listen.

Jabbar's decision caused quite a quandary. Gwenneth was bent on visiting Lusha to find out what he had told the authorities. But at the same time, not knowing Jabbar's exact plan made the predicament dangerous. Before she could make a decision two men came from around the corner, swords drawn.

"You are under arrest, by order of the Priest," the taller one said.

"On what grounds?" demanded Gwenneth.

"Witchcraft."

"Ridiculous! Witchcraft does not exist. Surely, the Priest can't believe in such things."

With the tip of his sword he touched her breastbone as he said, "It is not up to me to discuss what the Priest believes or does not believe. You are under arrest. You will come with me, or you will die now by this sword."

"If I am a witch, how could you arrest me? Would I not use my craft to escape?" challenged Gwenneth.

By the look on his face, the guard was not amused. He nodded to the shorter man who quickly came over and took my sister by force. He moved so fast that before I knew what was happening he had her hands tied behind her back.

"You brute, that hurt!" she snapped at him.

I didn't move, frozen in fear. My sister was so brazen I feared for her life. She was going to get us killed; I could feel it in my bones.

"She's next," said the tall one, pointing to me. The shorter man went behind me and tied my hands together. They walked behind us with their swords drawn at our backs. I thought about running, but both of them had very long legs and could surely outrun me. Besides, that would leave my sister behind, and if I did get away they would punish her for my actions.

We were taken to the tower. I wondered if Lusha knew we were there. Did he hear us come in, or was he held in another part of the tower? Did they detain Jabbar or did he get away? I hadn't seen him since he walked off. They put my sister and me together in the same room. It was dark, damp and smelled of human waste. We were each chained by the ankle in a separate corner of the room.

When the guard left, Gwenneth didn't waste any time telling me what to do.

"Do not admit to knowing anything," she whispered.

I didn't respond, so she continued, "We must stay alive at all costs. Never let them know the wand is a focus wand used for the sacred work. Deny everything."

"What will happen to Lusha?" I asked her.

I could hear her sigh deeply before answering me. "We can do nothing to help him. We must deny knowing anything about what he was doing. We must make them believe he was acting on his own."

It was hard to believe what she was demanding. "You want me to deny my husband and the sacred work?"

"There is no other way. There is no reason for us all to die. We must survive to carry on the work. The work is what is important, not our individual lives."

"No! I will not turn my back on him! Gwenneth, please, do not ask that of me. Is it not important for us to speak the truth and stand up for what we believe in?"

"Not at the risk of all of us being killed. We cannot carry on the sacred work if we are dead."

I was becoming more confused by the minute, swimming in emotional turmoil. I disagreed with her. I had a strong desire to stand up to all of them, even to her. I wanted to speak what I knew to be true. I was tired of living a life in secret. I was tired of the crazy world the worshippers lived in. I was… tired. I lay down on the cement floor and wept myself into a deep sleep.

I woke up when I heard a guard walk in. He came over and unlocked the chain around my ankle, grabbed my upper arm and yanked me to my feet.

"Where are you taking her?" Gwenneth shouted. "Leave her be!"

He didn't answer. I looked back at her as I was pushed through the doorway.

"Remember what I told you," she called. I wondered if I would ever see my sister again.

I was brought to a large room on the first floor of the tower. There, at a long table, the Priest sat with three men on one side, and four on the other. I had not seen any of these men before. The guard had me stand directly across the table from the Priest.

"State your name," the Priest said.

"Shriya. My name is Shriya, Shriya Cameret Adani."

"Do you know why you are here?"

"No."

"We have your husband. He was found with a magic wand. Such things are considered witchcraft. Witchcraft is the work of the Gatekeeper."

"I am not aware of any wand being magic," I answered honestly.

"Do you practice the work of the Gatekeeper?"

"No, I do not." I wanted to tell him how crazy this entire Gatekeeper idea was. I wanted to let him know how stupid it was to think any wand could be magic. I wanted to scream that the power of God lives in all of us. That each of us is divine by God's law. But I didn't. I kept hearing Gwenneth's words in my head, *Do not admit to knowing anything. We must deny knowing anything about what he was doing. We must make them believe that he was acting on his own.*

The Priest continued, "Were you aware of your husband's traveling plans? Did you know he carried a magic wand with him?"

"No," I lied. I continued to deny everything as Gwenneth wanted me to. But I kept thinking, if they are going to kill me anyway, why not tell them the truth? Why not tell them what the wand really was? Why not shatter the world as they know it? But I didn't. The Priest finally seemed satisfied by my answers.

"Let her go," he ordered. I assumed I was being taken back to the cell. I was wrong. I was being released.

As a precaution, I headed out of town before the Priest could change his mind. I had just set out on the road when I heard someone call my name. I stopped at the sound of the voice...a voice I knew. It sent shivers down my spine. Then I felt a hand touch the top of my shoulder.

"I heard you were in town. I also heard about Lusha."

I turned to face Parkin, and instinctively wrapped my arms around his neck, and buried my face in his chest. He held me tight as I sobbed and told him of my experience with the Priest. After several minutes I realized how this must look, and pushed myself away from his embrace, apologizing for my actions.

"Tears are a cleansing of the soul, Shriya," he said. "There is no need to apologize for them."

I looked up into his face and saw the compassion he had for me. "You need to remember," he continued, "Lusha made his choice. He knew the risks when he set out for this journey, not only the journey to deliver the wand, but the journey of his life. Remember, we will all live again."

"You are right. But it does not take away the pain of losing him in this lifetime. I have grown quite fond of him. He has been very kind to me. He does not deserve to have his life come to an end so soon," I said.

"No, he may not. But we live in a world which does not support the divinity in people. Therefore, anyone who knowingly practices any type of the ancient ways is aware of the risk he takes. You must trust he is serving his highest purpose."

How much knowledge Parkin had of the ancient ways, I did not know, so I was careful about saying too much on the subject. But on one thing he was right. I did need to trust my husband.

"Are you going home?" he asked.

"Yes, but they still have Gwenneth."

"Let me walk with you. There is nothing else you can do. After questioning her, I'm sure they will release her, too."

I think he saw the confusion on my face. I wanted him to walk me home although I knew it was improper. Even under these circumstances, I still yearned for him, and at last said, "Yes, please. I would like that very much."

We walked in silence for several minutes until I couldn't help myself, and had to ask him the question burning in my mind. "Parkin, do you think we will ever have a lifetime where we will be free? Free to speak the truth without worry of persecution? Free to love each other?"

His voice was tender as he answered, "I can only hope so, Shriya." He reached out and took my hand. We walked silently, hand in hand, the rest of the way. I could at last feel his essence in our physical contact, and relished every moment. I don't know if I would ever be able to accept that we could not be together. It seemed wrong to have such strong feelings and not be able to act on them.

When we reached the beginning of my road and my house was in sight, he stopped, embraced me, kissed me on the forehead and said, "Be well, Shriya, and be strong."

"I will," I promised. "I will."

As I walked to my house, I called Jumper. I needed comforting. My husband was being burned at sunset, yet my heart and mind were anchored to another man. What kind of person did this make me?

Jumper came bouncing along, happy to see me, his tail wagging as fast as it could go. I let him in the house so we could sit on the floor together and I could hold him. I thought it would make me feel better. It did, a little; but not as much as I had hoped. My mind raced, thinking about Lusha. I trembled when I thought about what it must be like to be burned. It seemed like a horrible death, and I feared if I did think about, I might draw a similar fate. I needed to keep busy and stop thinking. I'd go clean out the barn stalls. I hated that kind of work, but the other hate in my heart needed to be worked off. I hated the Priest, and I hated the worshippers for not accepting us, for being willfully ignorant of the truth, but most of all for being just plain ignorant.

It was getting dark, and I had expected Gwenneth hours ago, but she had still not returned. I paced back and forth, not knowing what to do. Should I go back into town or wait here? Light a candle? Look into the crystal ball? Fear took over my thinking, preventing me from making a decision one way or the other.

It was well after dark when Gwenneth finally arrived home. Her eyes were tear stained and her face blotchy and red. I had never seen her so upset. I knew Lusha was dead. I dropped to my knees and wept. She came over and put her arm around me.

"Jabbar is gone also." I looked up at her. Her voice was barely audible.

"They killed him while he was trying to break into the tower."

I held her as we both fell back to the floor and cried in each other's arms. I had lost my husband. She had lost the love of her life for a second time. It was a sad day.

CHAPTER TWENTY

THE NEXT TWO WEEKS WERE a blur. Gwenneth and I barely spoke to each other. Every night I was awakened by her crying. She was in deep emotional pain, but there wasn't anything I could do for her. I knew of no herbs, remedies or sacred knowledge to cure a broken heart. Only time could heal such wounds.

Gwenneth decided we should not go into town, and for once I agreed with her. It was best to stay away for a few months until things settled down. We would have to live with whatever supplies we had. We didn't expect any visitors for healings, the risk now was too great. I suspected even Janna was afraid to come. I now lived in fear of the townspeople and their worshipping ways. Lusha had always made me feel safe. He would never have let anyone or anything hurt me. I missed his comforting presence.

It was a gloomy day, but I decided to take Jumper for a walk anyway. Jumper ran ahead of me, as usual, but then to my surprise began to growl. He never growled or snarled so I stopped and listened, but didn't hear anything except Jumper, who by then was howling so loud he drowned out any other sounds. Taking no chances I hid behind a large tree and stayed hidden until I could figure things out. As Jumper got closer I was sure I also heard a human voice. I thought of the time Gwenneth was attacked by the Priest's son. Had the Priest sent one of his men to recapture me? I huddled close to the tree to make myself as invisible as possible, my heart pounding in my chest, my breathing loud enough to hear. Then Jumper appeared and gave away my hiding place. I heard footsteps following Jumper's path. I buried my face in the ground to avoid seeing what was coming next. It couldn't be good.

Strong hands rolled me over. I kept my eyes shut and screamed as loud as I could. I kicked and bit as hard as my strength would let me. My eyes flew open as I heard the words, "Shriya, it's me, Parkin. I won't hurt you." He jumped away from me as he let me go and stood with his feet apart and his arms open. "It's me. I thought you were hurt."

I sprang to my feet. "What are you doing here?" I screamed. "You scared me to death!"

"I came to see you." I looked up and saw sadness in his eyes I hadn't seen before. I calmed myself down.

"Parkin, is something wrong? Why are you here?"

"I must leave town. My father is sick and dying. As the oldest of four sons it is my responsibility to assume his role as head of my family. I won't be fishing any more or coming to town in my boat. My brothers will be responsible for our livelihood." He tried to continue, but the words got caught in his throat. He cleared it and began again. "I may never see you again, so I have come to say goodbye."

I'm not sure what got into me, but upon hearing this, I rose and put my arms around his neck. I brought his face to mine and kissed him passionately. As my lips touched his, I felt his energy travel through my body, and my insecurities vanished. My body ached for him. I wanted nothing less than to experience his essence and be with him completely, whatever the outcome. I pulled back and looked into his eyes as he gazed back into mine. Our lips met again, this time with even more fervor. Our souls struggled to become one, a complete and total energy exchange, intertwining us forever. There was no going back. My love for him was overpowering. It allowed me to be vulnerable enough to do what I wanted without worrying about the consequences. I knew I would never regret the decision.

Afterwards, he slept and I lay in his arms for a long time before slowly slipping out of his embrace. I sat quietly and watched him. A new energy, and an overwhelming love I had never known before flowed through my heart towards Parkin. I knew I had shocked him with my behavior, but I couldn't help myself. All my life I had done what was expected of me…but not this time. This time I acted for myself.

My reverie was broken by a soft snore. I wondered if I should wake him, but thought of the sorrow of saying goodbye and decided not to. I wanted my last memories of Parkin to be happy ones of him sleeping peacefully in the meadow. So I left him lying there and returned home.

CHAPTER TWENTY ONE

GWENNETH'S VISION CAME TO PASS. Several months later I was knitting baby clothes. Parkin's child was growing inside of me. Gwenneth was ecstatic and naturally assumed I was carrying Lusha's baby. She had taken the time to calculate when she thought the baby was due, and I hoped she wouldn't suspect anything when I was late delivering. She hounded me with questions about when the last time was that Lusha and I had been together. I did my best to avoid them, but finally decided to tell her it had been the last night he was home. If she became suspicious I could take some herbs to bring on birth contractions early. I hoped it wouldn't come to that as it could be risky for the baby.

I was as excited as Gwenneth was, but for a different reason. Part of Parkin would always be with me. I hoped for a boy, but it was too early to tell. They do say boys carry lower. Gwenneth had her own method of determining the child's sex. She held a pendulum over my belly. If it swung to the right I would surely have a boy...to the left, a girl. I found the procedure amusing because every time she tried it the pendulum moved in a different direction. But I let her have her fun. It was good to have some joy back in our lives. When I asked her why she didn't go to her crystal ball for the answer, she said she couldn't achieve the emotional detachment required for a true result.

As for me, I savored each stage of my pregnancy. I loved feeling the baby grow and move inside of me. It seemed to reflect the opposite of whatever activity I was engaged in...quietest when I was doing chores, most active when I was at my special meditation place. Gwenneth was ecstatic the bloodline would continue, and I let her believe it. She also suggested that if the baby was a boy he should be named Lusha after his father. I could never do that. Nor could I ever tell her why. I found it interesting that Gwenneth, who knew so much and could see into the future, never knew it was Parkin's baby. It proved to me that people see and believe what they want to, not necessarily what actually is true.

My belly got huge. I could hardly bend over, but I still cleaned out the stalls. My condition didn't keep Gwenneth from expecting me to maintain my share of the chores. We both felt Lusha's absence, not only in having to resume the work he had taken over, but also his kindness. I missed seeing his face every day. I even missed sleeping in his arms at night. I hadn't seen Parkin since the day we conceived our child...a secret I would take to my grave.

One day, as I swept old hay out of the barn, a hard, cramping pain in my lower torso stopped me where I stood. I was still six weeks away from the baby's due date, so I thought the pangs were from hunger. I stopped sweeping, went into the house, opened a jar of preserved peaches and ate some, then headed back outside. The pain came again, and this time it doubled me over. When the pain passed I made my way back to the house and lay down on my bed, sure the problem would disappear. But it didn't. I knew if the baby came this early there were sure to be complications with one or both of us. But the pain became more intense as the day went on. I had not seen Gwenneth all morning, but now I called for her. No answer. I thought she might be outside somewhere, so I sat up at the edge of the bed, preparing to go look for her, when I heard the door open.

It was Gwenneth. She entered with herbs in her hands. "Here I am," she said. "These will soothe your labor pains."

How did she know? Sometimes her ability was uncanny.

She helped me over to the healing table where we had saved so many lives. "Sit down here," she directed. "I'm going to prop up your back with bed pillows, and put some water to boil."

"But it is too early," I said.

"Babies come when they are ready to enter our world, not when we decide they should."

"Will it be alright, coming so early?"

"The crystal ball has shown me there is a problem. The birth cord is wrapped around the baby's neck. If steps are not taken to untangle it, she will die as she is born.

"She?"

"Yes. The baby is a girl."

"But what are we to do?"

"Do you recall when our nanny goat had so much trouble giving birth two years ago? Her unborn kid was in breach position, and would not come out. The nanny was exhausted from her labor, in great pain, and close to death. To save them both I had to reach inside her and turn the unborn animal, then help it out. I will do something similar for you when the time is ready. Your contractions will become stronger. Once you have the urge to push, you must tell me. It is then I will have to reach inside you, disentangle the cord, and pull the baby out. If you push without my assistance, the cord may strangle her."

I looked at Gwenneth in alarm, and then another pain came, this one more intense than the others. As the hours wore on, the pain became more than I thought I could bear. Just when I didn't think I could take any more, I announced loudly, "I need to push!"

Gwenneth soaped her hands, rinsed them in hot water and rushed over. I was so weak I was falling asleep between contractions. "Pull up your knees and open your legs!" she directed. I felt her hand slip in, and move to release the birth cord's grip on the baby's throat. When the next contraction came, she yelled, "Push!" I did and out slid my baby girl into Gwenneth's waiting hands. She grasped the baby around the ankles, turned her upside down, and patted her solidly on the back. The baby coughed up a small plug of mucus, and wailed at the insult, Gwenneth laughed with relief and placed her on my stomach. The baby was small since she was early, but everything else seemed to be alright. She was kicking already, and Gwenneth reassured me her body had a healthy glow.

I was exhausted as I looked at the bloody, messy, squirming body lying atop me. I had never seen anything so beautiful before. I put my hands around her and kissed the top of her wet bald head. Gwenneth cut the cord, tied it, and picked the baby up.

"I'll clean her up for you," she said." She took my little girl to the tub of water, gently bathed her and wrapped her snugly in a clean blanket I had knitted, and returned her to me.

"She is beautiful, Shriya, absolutely beautiful."

When I looked up at Gwenneth, I saw tears in her eyes. She was happy. I had fulfilled her dreams. Or so she thought.

I couldn't believe another human being had come out of me. It was an amazing thing to experience. I felt bad for Gwenneth; she would never personally know it. But we would enjoy raising this little girl together. I would name her Jasmine, after one of my favorite flowers. Jasmine would be the friend I never had. We would be close, and I would teach her everything I knew. We would adore each other, I was sure of it. And perhaps one day when she was older, we would run away together, find Parkin, and live as we were meant to….together at last. I had a lot of dreams.

Chapter Twenty Two

I watched Jasmine dig in the garden, looking for worms. She was fascinated by them and loved to play with the little things. She was four years old now, articulate and smart, but so strong willed that some days with her were a real challenge. There were times I had to remind myself I was the mother.

If I corrected her behavior, she acted as if I had just committed a crime against her. When she was just a toddler she had a bad habit of getting into the pottery garbage pail. She liked to go over to it, pull herself up and take things out of it. I would go over and remove her little hand and say, "no." She would look right at me with a defiant look and put her hand back in the pail with the intention of removing another piece of trash. We finally had to acquiesce to moving the garbage pail. It was just wasn't worth the fight.

Nevertheless, I loved being a mother, more than I could have imagined. Jasmine was the love of my life. She liked to snuggle at night. She would climb up in my lap and I would hold her while I told her stories. I invented special stories which included bits of the sacred knowledge, but were suitable for her understanding, to entertain her and enlighten her at the same time. I told tales about how fear controlled certain animal kingdoms from reaching their fullest potential. I told stories about two people in love conceiving a child out of that love. I told stories about a lion not wanting his brother to fall in love with a tiger because he believed the lions must keep their bloodlines pure. I told stories to relieve my own burden of guilt. Most importantly, I told stories my little girl would someday understand the true meaning of.

Jasmine had long, blond, curly hair. My father had curly blond hair and so did Lusha. My sister and I took after my mother. I was fortunate Jasmine took after my father's side, for everyone assumed she was Lusha's child. As far as I knew, my lie was safe.

Jasmine loved to pick flowers. We would walk through the meadow picking all we could find. But her favorites were the daisies which grew in abundance around our home. She would pick them and put them in her hair. One day I put some in my hair. She became agitated, and cried, "No, only me, only me!" She came over and took the daisies out of my hair but left the pink carnations I had put there. She frowned at me and said again, "Only me."

Jasmine relished drama. I can't recount how many times she pretended to be sick to get my attention. Of course, it never worked with Gwenneth since she could see the energy field around my precious child. But I wouldn't listen to my sister; I coddled Jasmine and gave her all my attention when she played sick. I made special teas for her to drink, and sat with her for hours.

One day Gwenneth came to me and said, "You have to stop giving in to Jasmine when she pretends. It does not serve her well when you do."

"But she must need me if she goes to such lengths to get my attention," I argued.

"It is her way of manipulating you, and you succumb to it every time," Gwenneth retorted. I assumed she was jealous because she wasn't able to have a child, and ignored her advice.

Jasmine loved her aunt and her aunt loved her back in equal measure, if not more. When she was learning how to speak, she could not pronounce the name Gwenneth. So she called her "Wenny". My sister loved the pet name. In return Gwenneth called my little one "Jasi".

Jasmine has a special way with animals. Many of the small creatures who lived around our home allowed her to pick them up and pet them. They would play with her and let her chase them until she became overtired and started to cry. Then they left, disturbed by her outbursts.

One sunny, warm day Jasmine and I decided to go out for a walk. As we strolled towards the lake, I smelled the perfume of jasmine flowers in the air. I pointed the bushes out to her and told her how she got her name.

"I am named after a flower?" she asked.

"My favorite flower. Can you smell their perfume?"

She pressed her nose in the middle of the white flowers and inhaled deeply.

"Umm....".

"Aren't they intoxicating?" I asked.

"What is toxicatty?"

"I n t o x i c a t i n g," I repeated slowly.

"If that means they smell real good, yes, I think they are toxicating!" She smiled and all her upper teeth showed.

I laughed as I took her hand and we continued to walk to the lake. When we got there I spread out the blanket I had brought along. We lay in the sun looking up at the clouds, trying to distinguish recognizable shapes. "Look!" I exclaim. "A bunny in the clouds."

"I see it, too!" Jasmine squealed with delight. "And there's a lady's face, right over there." She pointed, but I had to admit I couldn't find it.

"Where?" I asked her.

"That cloud, the one right in front of us, Mama. Right there!"

I continued to look where she pointed and began to see two almond shaped eyes looking at me. I vaguely heard my daughter say, "Look Mama! The face is coming alive." I saw it then. The face became larger and closer to us. I was about to grab Jasmine and run, when I heard in my head, *"Do not be afraid. Always remember, others will reflect back to you what you need to learn. If you see fear in others, look inside yourself."* Then the face slowly dissolved, melting before my eyes.

"Mama, Mama! Did you see that?" She poked me to get my attention. I hesitantly looked over at her and shook my head to snap myself to attention.

"Yes, Jasmine, I saw it. Did you hear anything?"

"No, Mama. Was I supposed to?"

"I thought I heard something, that's all." I sat up, determined to leave. "Well, I do believe it's time to go home."

"So soon? We haven't even gone swimming yet."

I stood up, reached for her hand and plucked her from the blanket. Something in my face must have warned her not to create a fuss.

Jasmine and I headed home. I was lost in thought as Jasmine ran ahead of me. The face I saw in the cloud was the same one I had seen materialize out of the lake so many years ago. I was sure of it. I wanted to get home and think about the message I'd been given, but that wasn't to be. I heard Jasmine yelling.

"Mama, come quick!"

I ran to catch up to her, afraid of what I would find. Jasmine was crouched down on the ground holding a tiny bunny in her hands. She looked up at me when I arrived by her side.

"He's hurt, Mama. We have to help him. Can we heal him Mama, can we?"

"Of course we can."

I sat down next to her, picked the bunny up and held it in my hands. She placed her little hands over the top of the bunny. I watched her close her eyes. I could tell by the look on her face that she was trying to concentrate. She was putting her mind into a trance. She was focusing on allowing God's love to flow through her to heal this tiny animal. I also closed my eyes and we both unconditionally loved this bunny to health.

We both opened our eyes at the same time. Our work was done. I was wondering what we should do with the bunny, when all of a sudden I felt other eyes upon us.

"Jasmine, I think we are being watched. The bunny's mother must be near. Let us leave the bunny here. We will hide behind the bushes and see if the Mama comes to get her baby."

We hid ourselves behind a nearby bush, and waited for only a few seconds before the eyes that were watching us appeared out of nowhere. It was a hawk! In a moment it swooped down and grasped the bunny in its talons. Horrified, we looked at each other and screamed as we watch the hawk and its prey disappear into the sky.

Chapter Twenty Three

After Lusha was killed, I took my focus wand and buried it. At the Priest's inquiry I had turned my back on Lusha, pretending I knew nothing of the sacredness of the wand. I hoped to relieve my guilt by acting as if my false testimony was true. I forced myself to see the wand as nothing more than a decorated stick, a stick that caused death, a stick I would never use again.

Instead, I put all my concentration into seeing the future. I wanted to be able to protect my little girl from any harm coming her way. I looked into my crystal ball every night after she fell asleep. But there were times when I couldn't change what I saw. Some things needed to play out for her to learn on her own. Like the time I saw her sneak up on a squirrel and grab it by the tail. I saw the squirrel twist around and bite her. The next morning I gave her another lecture about respecting the animals when they had babies to protect. She had an unusual ability with small creatures, and I had become accustomed to sick animals finding their way to our home for healings. But Jasmine could walk up to almost any animal and pick it up, hold it, pet it, and then put it back down as if it were a household pet. It used to worry me until I finally accepted she had a special way with them. But she never seemed to grasp that when a female had babies, she should keep her hands off.

It was spring and newborn animals were abundant. I turned my back only for a moment when I heard her scream. I turned to see her holding her finger up to her mouth.

"It bited me!" she wept ruefully.

Since I had seen it the night before in my crystal ball, I knew immediately what had happened. I rushed over to her and pulled her hand out of her mouth. She cried even louder. Gwenneth came running out of the house.

"It's nothing," I said. "She tried to grab a mama squirrel and was bitten."

"It bited me," Jasmine screamed again so her aunt could hear.

Gwenneth corrected her, "It bit you. There is no such word as bited, and you shouldn't bother a mother animal. Any mama will protect her young."

Jasmine was not pleased with Gwenneth's apparent lack of concern. She looked at me. "It bited…." She stopped and reformed her words. "It bit me."

"Next time, ask permission of the animal before you touch it," I said.

She thought for a moment. "Well, I suppose it is only fair. Animals have a soul, too. Don't they?"

"Yes, they do. A soul exists in all living things."

I could see the wheels spin in her little head.

"Well," she said. "Then the squirrel should have known I wouldn't hurt it!" She turned and walked off defiantly.

I had to smile. She was such a stubborn little thing, and in many ways took after my sister. I loved Jasmine so much…more than I could have believed possible. The love of a mother is probably the closest thing to unconditional love. But something else caused me to have great concern for Jasmine. What if I wasn't around to raise her? Of course, if anything happened to me, she would have Gwenneth. But I didn't want Jasmine to be raised to believe she must live her life to serve humanity. I wanted her to grow up free in every way. Free to love whomever she wanted. Free to live her life as she chose. The vision in the cloud seemed to be addressing this. I couldn't let go of it, and it consumed me.

CHAPTER TWENTY FOUR

DECEMBER 1559

Jasmine was growing up quickly, too fast for my own liking. On December 21st, she turned twelve. Because her birthday is on the winter solstice, we had a double celebration. It didn't take long for me to realize I didn't much care for twelve-year-olds. She became sassy and difficult to get along with, ready to argue about everything. I could ask her to scrub out a pot or two, and she would find some reason why it was unreasonable of me to ask it of her.

The truth was, I didn't understand her anymore. She was constantly trying to boss me around. What had happened to my darling little girl? She didn't give Gwenneth nearly as much trouble. But I noticed Gwenneth removed herself from the conflict between my daughter and me. One day I confronted my sister about it.

"You see how stubborn she is, don't you?" I asked Gwenneth.

"Yes, very stubborn. She has a strong will."

"There are times when I could use your help." I could feel the desperation in my voice.

"How so?"

"You could back me up, show you support me."

"You seem to be doing fine on your own, Shriya."

"No, I am not doing fine. I can't understand how she has gotten this way."

"Sister, it is your fate. You must work it out yourself. Have you thought about looking into her past, to see what issues she brought with her?"

"No, it never occurred to me I could."

"Well, you can. Simply gaze into your looking glass, and with Jasmine's past life as a target allow your mind to go into a trance. It will take you back to the past and show you who she has been."

"Have you done this? Do you know about her past?"

"No, it is not my place to do so. Jasmine is your daughter. I suspect it is something the two of you must work out."

I was excited about the possibility, and remembered Aunt Kalini telling me how she had used the technique to learn what transpired between the Priest and my mother's spirit after mother had been burned at the stake. I had forgotten about it long ago, never considering I could use the same method to see my daughter's previous lifetimes. Maybe it would allow me to understand my child better.

I waited until Jasmine was asleep. In our small house it was hard to do anything secretly. I dressed warmly and headed outside to the barn with looking glass and burning candle in hand, and made myself comfortable next to the bundles of hay, careful not to come close enough to catch the hay on fire.

I settled in and looked deep into the heart of the flame as I went into a trance with my daughter's past as my focus, then turned my gaze from flame to the looking glass. First I saw myself looking back, but gradually my own face faded and other faces came and went. Soon I was looking at only one face, the face of a young princess. She sat on a throne wearing a beautiful headdress of daisies. The image disappeared. I tried to bring it back, but nothing would come.

I sat for a while trying to understand what I had seen. Why was there a throne? What culture practiced royalty? The Priest and his family had been in control for centuries. How far back had I seen? Then I remembered. The island tribesmen still had royal families who at one time ruled the island, but no more. When their sailboats began regular visits to the mainland, the Priest didn't waste any time using his power to control them, and soon their families and kings, as well. Now the status of royal families was merely symbolic. The royals were powerless, but admired for their beauty. Like us, they functioned under the rule of the Priest

So Jasmine had been a princess of the island. It made sense. My daughter was Parkin's daughter, too, and he was an island tribesman. I was used to thinking of Jasmine as solely ours, but she was not. Her blood was a mixture of the tribesmen line as well as our own sacred line. I wondered how much her soul remembered her past life. I only hoped her imperious royal attitude would not offer clues to give my secret away. It would destroy Gwenneth.

I walked back to the house and went to bed. I looked at my beautiful daughter as she slept. As I watched, I recalled her taking the daisies off my head when she was only four years old. I didn't know much about the tribesmen, their rituals or their royalty, but I made an assumption that only royalty wore a crown of daisies.

CHAPTER TWENTY FIVE

IT WAS A CLOUDY DAY and Jasmine was outside playing. Nothing stopped her need to be in contact with nature. It was hard to keep her in, even when it was raining, as she wasn't bothered by any type of weather. In that and other ways she was a lot like me. Gwenneth and I watched her out the window. She was getting taller all the time; her thirteenth birthday would be coming up soon. I thought as she got older, her love for animals would diminish, but instead it got stronger. She wasn't as skilled at healing as Gwenneth and I, but seemed better able to communicate with the domestic and wild creatures. Many times she was the first to know if a nearby animal needed food, healing, or help.

On one occasion she insisted the nanny goat was going to deliver that night. My sister and I laughed at her. We knew the goat wasn't due for at least another two weeks. Jasmine argued with us, and decided to sleep out in the barn with the pregnant goat.

Late that night the goat went into labor. Jasmine was there for the birth. In the morning, I found her lying beside the nanny and her newborn kid, with dried blood and birthing fluid on her arms. She had personally assisted the baby goat into his new world.

After that, Gwenneth and I listened to what she had to say and it frequently helped us. The animals seemed to know in advance what nature was about to unleash upon us. Through Jasmine we were warned of upcoming storms. Animals had the natural sixth sense we were trying to cultivate through practice of the sacred arts.

Fall arrived, blowing leaves off the trees and bringing colder, stormy weather. It was one of my favorite times of the year, a time when Mother Nature alerts us to get ready, like the plants and animals, to dream a new, winter dream. We stay indoors and sleep more as the nights get longer. The darkness and quiet give us an opportunity to contemplate and dream about what we would like to accomplish in the coming seasons. I loved this frosty dream time, and decided to use it to teach Jasmine more about our bond with nature.

I called Jasmine in from outside, and though the wind was blowing the rain almost horizontal, she was reluctant to do so. "Go dry off," I urged her. "Then come and sit in front of the fire. I have a story to tell you."

Jasmine removed her wet clothing, wrapped herself in a blanket and settled before the hearth. "This storm reminds me of a great lesson your aunt taught me when I was about your age. What does nature do in winter?" I asked her.

"Well, it snows, it's cold, and the animals hibernate."

"Exactly, but what do the plants do?"

"They don't do anything. They are dead."

"They only appear to be dead," I replied. "They are actually in hibernation. Hibernation is a time for the plants to dream what they want to become the next spring. They are putting their dream into the ether field, but so subtly we humans cannot detect it until we achieve a certain amount of mastery ourselves. That is why we never disturb the plants and trees during winter. We do not want to interrupt their dream. Winter is also a time for us to dream what we want for the next year. A time to be contemplative and to start affecting the energy field with that dream."

"Then nature takes us into spring. What does nature do in the spring time?"

"Spring is a time when everything starts to come alive again. The flowers poke out from the ground, and grasses and trees turn green again," Jasmine replied.

"Yes, spring is about coming alive, springing into action. It is a time for us to put into action a plan on how to achieve our new dream. To function at our best we should be in tune with the seasons, so it is also when we start to renew ourselves after being indoors during the coldest season."

Jasmine nodded.

"What season comes after spring?"

"Summer, of course."

"Think about the weather. After the plants get their buds, what do they do next?"

"They bloom."

"What causes them to bloom?"

"The sun, I suppose."

"Summer is the time when nature lives its new dream to the fullest."

"And can we live our lives in full bloom, too?" Jasmine asked.

"Yes. We bloom in spirit, like all of nature, by living our dream to its fullest." I stopped so she could really think about my words. "Summer is the most active time for nature. There are more daylight hours, more sunshine. Animals stay out longer. Bees are busy pollinating the fruit trees. The caterpillars have transmuted themselves into butterflies by creating cocoons and dreaming a new dream of flying. We are also most active during the summer, enjoying the long summer days like the rest of the natural world. This is when our previous winter's dream has come to pass. We get to enjoy the fruits of our labor as we are busy living our dream. Everything has now manifested."

"I like all the seasons," she said defiantly. "Not just summer."

I could see I had somehow offended her, and made a mental note to soften my approach.

"And well you should," I responded with a smile. "Each season has its own beauty and importance. In autumn we harvest our garden and put food up for the winter. The animals forage for the winter, many of them storing up food for the lean times. Harvesting is about gaining wisdom from having lived our dream to its fullest. It is about letting go of any mistakes we may have made along the way. Even leaves let go, and fall off the trees. Hopefully we can let go of all the grief or worry we experienced and bring only the wisdom we have gained into the next year. That completes Mother Nature's natural cycle of life."

I believed Jasmine was absorbing the lesson. I had lived my life in accordance to these precepts without even knowing it, and it had served me well. I hoped it would do the same for her.

"Do you understand my meaning, Jasmine?"

"Yes, yes I do!" she said enthusiastically. "I think I've always lived this way but never considered why until now. On many of my birthdays, I thought about what my year had been like. Thank you, Mama. Thank you for explaining it to me."

She reached over and hugged me. I was delighted. She didn't usually volunteer hugs anymore. I was lucky to get one when I tucked her into bed at night with a loving nighttime ritual I wasn't ready to give up. First, I'd rub her back, then I would have her turn over, and would place my hands on her head as I said this prayer:

Oh My Beloved God, protect this child from harm.
Enrich her life that she may know your work directly.
Guide her mind so that she makes wise decisions that will enhance her life.
Fill her with your divine light. So Be It.

As far as I was concerned she would never be too old for that.

The next morning, the storm had subsided. Jasmine was outside doing chores. I was cleaning up the table after breakfast and Gwenneth was nearby. "We need to start planning Jasmine's thirteenth birthday," I said. "Before we know it, December will be upon us."

"One thing has already been planned," Gwenneth said. "A former friend of Jabbar has taken over the practice of making focus wands. He has been working on Jasmine's wand, and will travel here to present it to her."

I spun around so fast it made me a little dizzy. "She will not have a wand. I forbid it!"

"You forbid it?"

"That is what I said. No more wands in this family. They have brought nothing but frustration and harm to us and those we loved."

"Shriya," Gwenneth said patiently, "you are not being reasonable. The wand is essential in her training. You know the importance of it."

"I know no such thing."

"You are not in a position to forbid it. She is to carry on the sacred work. In order to do this, she must receive her wand. It is tradition."

"I am her mother," I said, my voice rising as I spoke. "I make the decisions regarding her, not you."

"Shriya, calm down. There is no need to be angry."

"I will calm down when you agree I am her mother and have all rights to her welfare. I make all decisions regarding her, not you!"

"Up to this point, that has been true. But you do not have the right to deny her the next step in the sacred work. It is her divine right." Gwenneth was speaking softly now which really irritated me. I wanted her to yell back, I did not want her to try and reason with me.

I stood there and stared at her as she continued, "Take some time to think about it. You need to give her every opportunity to excel. Humanity depends upon us."

"And if I refuse?" I asked defiantly.

"You will leave us no choice but to take her from you."

"What do you mean, take her from me? You wouldn't dare!"

"I'm sure it will not come to that. I have no doubt you will find it in your heart to honor your agreement."

"What agreement?"

"The agreement you made on a soul level; the agreement to carry on the work, no matter what."

I was so tired of listening to this kind of talk I snapped, "There is no agreement! You make this up because you have can't have children of your own. You use me to fulfill your own dreams!"

Gwenneth's jaw dropped and she looked away. As soon as I said it, I wished I hadn't. I believed what I said was true, but I didn't need to say it. I could tell it hurt her deeply.

She got up and wordlessly walked off. I didn't see her again until the next morning. You could feel the tension in the room. Jasmine noticed it as soon as she got up. "What's going on? What's wrong?" she asked.

Before I could think of what to say Gwenneth answered, "Your mother does not want you to have a focus wand. She would rather have your energy drop than give you the tool to keep your mind focused on the sacred work. Once your energy drops, you may not be able to see into the other dimensions, your abilities may be limited."

Her statement made the heat rise in my body. Jasmine looked confused.

"That is not true," I said through clenched teeth. I looked at Jasmine. "My first concern is to protect you. I cannot protect you if you have an illegal item. A focus wand could bring about your death. I will not risk it."

"But isn't almost everything about us illegal?" she asked.

"That is not the point. There is to be no more discussion about this."

I stormed out of the house and scared Jumper who had been sleeping outside the door. He had become old and didn't roam the woods as often as he used to. His gallop had become more of a slow, deliberate walk. I knew his days were numbered and I was waiting for Jasmine to tell me when he was going to leave us for good. I would miss him. But right now I was consumed with anger toward my sister. Gwenneth had often pushed me to the edge, but this time she went too far. I would never forgive her for speaking to my daughter as she did about a decision that was mine to make.

I shook with anger as I ran to my special place by the lake. I stood at the edge of the lake and cried out, "Oh, my beloved God, help me!" I sank to my knees, hung my head low and wept. Gwenneth had betrayed me. I had tried to live up to her expectations, and this was how she repaid me. I would not let her get away with it.

As I looked out over the lake, I saw the same mist I had seen so many years ago as a child. The mist once again started to take form and appeared to me as the Lady of the Mist.

"*I am here to help you,*" I heard. "*I know all things.*"

"What do you want of me?" I asked.

"*It is not what I want; it is what you want. If it is not in your heart to dedicate your life to serve others, does it do any good to live the lie?*"

I gasped. Was I supposed to feel guilty? I had dedicated my life to the work; I had married the man Gwenneth chose for me. It was not my fault

I had not conceived a child with Lusha. I had done all the right things, except........ I had conceived a child with Parkin.

"Your child was conceived out of pure love. There is no reason to feel guilty."

Was the statement meant to comfort me? It didn't. I was alarmed that someone or something knew what I had done.

"All information in the ether energy field can be accessed, if desired," the being said.

I hoped that didn't mean Gwenneth knew who Jasmine's true father was.

"Does it matter what she knows or what she thinks? This is your life to live."

Yes, I thought. This is my life, not Gwenneth's. I cannot be responsible for what happened to her all those years ago. It is sad she has not been able to fulfill her destiny, but it does not mean I have to fill it for her. Humbly I said, "Thank you, Lady of the mist." I bowed in reverence.

The mist dissolved back into a fog which floated above the lake. I felt renewed, with fresh insight. I knew what I must do. I would run away with my daughter and take her to the island of the tribesmen.

Chapter Twenty Six

Jasmine woke me early in the morning. "Mama, Mama, wake up."

I opened my eyes to see her standing above me. "What is it?" I asked.

"It's Jumper, he wants to say goodbye. He is leaving us today."

"What? What do you mean?" In my heart I knew what she meant. Jumper was old. I could see it in him every day. He no longer romped through the woods like he used to, but lay for hours outside the door. He grimaced in pain as he walked. It had been obvious for months. I hated to acknowledge it. He had been such a large part of my life. I didn't want him to go.

"Jumper is leaving us. It is his time. He has worn out his body," Jasmine continued.

I sat up in bed and looked down on the floor. Jumper was sitting there looking at me. He wagged his tail as he came and licked my face. I usually didn't allow it, but this time I closed my eyes and let myself feel his energy as his tongue washed my face. I opened my eyes and said to him, "You have been a wonderful pet and companion. I have loved you greatly. Thank you for being in our lives. I will miss you. We will all miss you." Tears slid down my cheeks as he turned around and limped outside. We never saw him again.

The day was about loss. I lost my animal companion of many years. I was about to lose my sister. She didn't know it yet, but I was leaving and taking Jasmine with me. I would not allow Gwenneth to steal her from me in any way.

That night, when I was sure Gwenneth was sound asleep, I shook Jasmine gently, and whispered, "Wake up. We are going on a journey. We'll be taking our things. Get up and get dressed. But be quiet, we don't want to wake your aunt."

Jasmine didn't move.

"Didn't you hear me? Get up. We have a great journey ahead of us."

"What kind of journey?"

"An adventure. Now get up and get dressed. I'll answer questions later."

She grudgingly acquiesced.

We made our way to town. I had looked into the crystal ball earlier and seen several boats in dock. Most importantly, I had seen Parkin's family boat. He would not be on it, but one of his brothers would. I was sure I could persuade him to take us to the island. If I had to, I would tell him about Parkin's child.

Jasmine asked me several questions, but I kept my answers short. I told her only that we were on an adventure. She was so excited with the idea of being away from home she didn't give me any trouble. Our lives had been very sheltered. Other than monthly visits to town, she had never been anywhere else.

When we arrived in town, I took her to the docks. I pointed to Parkin's family boat. "How would you like to go for a boat ride to an island?"

"I have never been on a boat," she said with enthusiasm, "and I would like it very much."

"I haven't been on one either. But I thought it was time for us to do it. Wait here. I need to see who is in charge.'

I walked over to the boat and could see a lamp in the window below the deck. I knocked on the window. No one answered so I knocked again.

"Yes?" I heard a loud voice.

I didn't know what to say, so I knocked again.

"What do you want?"

"I would like to speak with you."

"Who are you?"

"You don't know me. My name is Shriya. I know Parkin."

Sounds of movement came from below the deck. Soon a man emerged.

"Well, what brings you to disturb me at this time of night?" he asked gruffly.

"I would like to hire you to take me and my daughter to your island." I removed a small fabric pouch from a hidden pocket in my cloak, opened it and proffered several coins. His glance showed me he was not impressed by the sum.

"What for?"

"To visit Parkin. He is an old friend and I have not seen him for many years."

He looked me up and down, then gestured towards Jasmine. "Who's she?"

"This is my daughter, Jasmine."

I expected he would introduce himself at that point, but he didn't. Instead he appeared to consider my offer. The long silence made me uncomfortable. At last he said, "You may come aboard."

"Thank you," I breathed a sigh of relief, and held the money out to him once more.

"Keep your coins. I do not want them," he said. He extended a hand and helped us aboard. "You can stay in the cabin where it is warm." He looked into my eyes and answered the question he saw there.

"Tomorrow we will sail on the morning tide."

Chapter Twenty Seven

W^{E WERE ON OUR WAY} at sunrise. It was a magical morning. A glowing pink covered the sky, and reflected brightly across the surface of the water. I hoped it was an indication of what I could expect on the rest of this adventure.

Jasmine did well on the boat. It was fun to watch her as she witnessed sea life for the first time. She was on the alert for any creature that plied the waters, and would shriek with delight when she saw a fish jump.

Parkin's brother was a man of few words. He still had not told us his name. So I passed the time watching my daughter enjoy her journey as I daydreamed about Parkin. He was sure to be married by now, and perhaps even had children of his own. I wondered if I should tell him Jasmine was his daughter. I would have to wait and see how things went. I intended to tell him about my fight with my sister regarding the focus wand. Once he heard it, he might take pity and arrange for Jasmine and me to stay somewhere on the island. I was prepared to work. I had many talents I could use to provide for us, and was willing to cook and clean for others if I had to.

By the time we saw land again, the sun was directly overhead. And even though the sea had occasionally been choppy, other than a sore bottom, I had been feeling well. But now that we were nearing the island I became sick to my stomach. The thought of seeing Parkin again overwhelmed me. I bent over, prepared to throw up.

Parkin's brother looked at me. "Now you're getting sick?" he said with a wry smile.

"I'm not sure what has come over me," I lied. I started to panic. I had no idea what to expect upon landing. I wasn't familiar with the tribesmen's customs. I had acted in anger without thinking things out. It was too late to worry about that now. We were about to dock.

I closed my eyes and silently prayed, "My beloved God, be with me this day and guide me in the right direction." I opened my eyes. Just beyond the large dock was a village where men and women bustled about and children ran and played. I could already feel a sense of joy coming from it. Excitement and nervousness took over again as I continued to look on.

Parkin's brother had already pulled down the sail. Now he let the boat's momentum ease it into the dock. When it gently bumped the landing, he jumped off and tied it to a pole with a strong rope.

"Wait here," he said, and walked away. I stood up to stretch my legs and almost fell over. My legs had become weak and wobbly. I sat back down, weary from the ride, and could see Jasmine become impatient now we were back on land. She was anxious to explore the village. I explained we had to be patient until we were given further instructions.

"We must wait here. We are not familiar with the customs of these people. We want to make sure we are respectful and honor them in their ways. I'm sure the captain will be back soon."

Jasmine asked, "What if he never comes back? What will we do then? Are we going to sit here forever?"

I laughed. "No, we will not sit here forever. I'm sure they will need their boat again." Jasmine rolled her eyes. She did not appreciate my sense of humor.

"Here he comes, Mama. And he is bringing another man."

I felt my heart race as I turned around to see who was with him. My heart sank in disappointment. The man was short, stocky, and bald. They approached the boat together, and Parkin's brother said, "Come." He reached his hand out to steady me. "You must go with this man."

"Who is he?" I asked.

"He is a guard of the island."

"But I came to see Parkin."

"You must go with the guard first. Permission must be granted for you to see my brother."

"Permission from whom?"

"Never mind. You must follow the guard."

Jasmine jumped out of the boat as if she was afraid I was going to leave her behind. We followed the guard through the open square where children raced after one another in pure joy. Jasmine watched them with amusement. Neither Jasmine nor I had ever had children to play with, so I hoped someday she would be accepted as one of them.

We were escorted to a great building made of limestone, the largest building I had ever seen, towering over everything around it. A brick pathway led to the roofed entryway, which was lined with potted plants. I had never seen plants in pots before. Inside the building was a large central room with more potted plants and furniture adorned with metal. It was beautiful. Both Jasmine and I stared in amazement. We were directed to take a seat, and once we had done so, the guard disappeared through a nearby doorway.

In his absence we let our eyes devour the exquisite surroundings. The place was richly furnished; the furnishings adorned with ornate metal, beautiful handwork in colorful and gold and silver threads, even jewels. Everything in the room spoke of great wealth and skilled craftsmanship.

The guard returned. "The king will see you now," he said, and motioned for us to rise.

"The king?" Jasmine asked.

I shushed her, but was thinking the same thing. I didn't realize we would need the king's permission to speak to Parkin.

We followed the guard again, this time into a small, windowless room lit by the blaze of many candles. At home, windows and an open door were our basic source of light during the day. Candles were a commodity not to be used frivolously.

We took our seats and waited patiently. I was nervous about meeting a king. But I wasn't nearly as nervous as I would be when I was able to see Parkin again. We sat there for some time until I heard the door to the room open. I didn't know what a king should look like, but considering the opulence of this building I expected him to be very impressive. He came closer and I was speechless, unprepared for what I saw. He walked quickly over to me, took both my hands and looked into my eyes. I barely let out a whisper.

"Parkin?" I said.

"Shriya, it has been such a very long time," he replied.

"Parkin?" I whispered again, scarcely believing my eyes.

"Yes." He let go of my hands and embraced me, "I have missed you."

"Oh, Parkin, you have no idea how much I've missed you!" Relief washed over me. I wanted to stay in his arms forever. Then I glanced over and saw my daughter watching us. I released his embrace.

"Parkin, allow me to introduce you to my daughter." I motioned for her to come over. She timidly moved in my direction. I put my arm around her shoulder.

"Jasmine, this is Parkin, a very dear and old friend of mine."

"Parkin, this is my daughter, Jasmine."

Parkins eyes went wide, he looked over at me. I smiled at him. He bowed to her and said, "It's an honor to meet you."

Jasmine bowed in return and said, "I am honored, as well."

I was standing in between the two most important people in my life. It was like a dream.

"What brings you to the island? Has something happened?" Parkin asked.

I looked at Jasmine. I couldn't talk openly about the fight with my sister in front of my daughter. He smiled as if acknowledging my predicament. I quickly changed the subject.

"We were told we had to meet the king. No one told me it was you." I hesitated. "You are the king, aren't you?"

"I am the royal king of the island," he replied.

"You never told me," I said.

"I told you my father was sick, and I had to come home and assume his responsibilities."

"But you never mentioned your father was the king. I thought you were a fishing family?"

"We are. We also carry the royal bloodline of the island." I sat back down. My legs had begun to wobble again.

Parkin looked at Jasmine. "You must be hungry." He reached up and pulled a braided cord that rang a loud bell. A man immediately appeared. "Please take this young woman to the kitchen, and fix her a nice meal. She must be famished. And have someone bring us some tea and food as well." He turned to me and said, "We have a lot to discuss."

CHAPTER TWENTY EIGHT

Parkin and I sat down together. I must have looked distressed for he clasped both of my hands and said, "Shriya, what is it?"

"I have so much to tell you. I don't where to begin," I said.

"Start by telling me why you are here."

I told him about my fight with Gwenneth; how strongly I felt about Jasmine not participating in the practice of a focus wand. I reminded him it had caused Lusha's death, and had instigated my rejection of anything to do with the wand. He listened patiently to everything.

When I finally stopped talking he said, "I understand how you feel. Jasmine's father was killed because of the wand. It is only natural you would want to protect her from the same fate."

"Yes," I said in a whisper. "Lusha was killed because of it." I couldn't look him in the face as I said this. I couldn't tell him about his daughter. Not yet.

"Jasmine and I need a safe place to stay. I do not want to live with my sister any longer. I am tired of her trying to control me and my daughter.

"You may stay here on the island. However, I need to warn you. Outsiders are not easily accepted. The villagers are a close knit group. Outsiders are only accepted when they marry a tribesman."

That statement reminded me to ask, "How is your wife?"

"My wife died in labor for our first child."

"I am so sorry, Parkin. I didn't know."

"It's alright. It was a long time ago. I am happy you have a child. It is something I have always longed for."

"Did the child not survive?" I asked with great concern.

"No, my child died, too."

"Oh, what a heartbreaking loss! You have my deepest sympathies."

"Thank you. Now let us find you and your daughter a place to stay. We have a number of guest rooms in the palace. You can stay here for now."

He wrapped his arms around me and kissed me on the cheek before he turned and left.

Jasmine and I were shown into a beautiful room with a big window overlooking the sea. We were exhausted from the long boat ride and I was emotionally drained from the excitement of seeing Parkin. Tired as I was, I couldn't take a nap. I lay awake thinking of Parkin. His wife and child had died. Should I tell him about Jasmine? It would be difficult to tell someone a secret you've kept for so many years. What purpose would it accomplish? Would he believe me? Hate me for keeping it from him? My mind raced with questions for which I had no answers. I tossed and turned for over an hour. I rolled over and looked at my sleeping daughter. She had Parkin's nose and mouth, but otherwise looked like my father's side of the family. Her blonde curly hair hung in her face as she dozed.

I wondered what Gwenneth thought when she woke up and discovered we were gone. She had underestimated me. As I turned the incidents over in my mind I began to feel angry again, but tried to let it go. I refocused my thoughts on Parkin and allowed myself to daydream about what it would be like to live here with him. I felt joy wash over me and liberate my body with a new state of mind; love. I had always been in love with him. It was time I told him.

A servant came with gowns for us. We were to dress for dinner. Jasmine was overjoyed. She had never worn anything so luxurious. My actions had robbed her of the opportunity to celebrate her thirteenth birthday with the sacred rituals. She would never wear a celebration gown. So I was happy to see her excited. The gown, a light green with a high neckline and fitted waist, suited her. The color was lovely against her blonde hair.

My gown was deep blue, fitted under my bosom to accent my breasts. I had never worn a gown that did such a thing. But I loved the way I looked in it. For the first time in my life I no longer felt like the plain looking girl who longed to fit in.

We were both excited and nervous. Neither one of us ever imagined putting on special clothes to eat a meal. We were taken to a special room where there was a large table set about with many chairs. Parkin was already sitting at the far end of the table when we came in. I was directed to sit on his right and Jasmine on his left. A servant bowed as he said to Parkin, "Will there by anything else?"

"We are ready for the food now," Parkin replied.

The servant left and returned with two others carrying plates of foods I had never seen before. Jasmine clapped her hands in delight, and Parkin laughed at her excitement. We had all manner of strange sea creatures and plants. Nothing looked familiar, but everything was delicious.

Every time I looked over at Parkin his gaze was on me. I got so nervous I lost my appetite. However, Jasmine consumed everything she could. I had never seen her eat so much at one sitting. I found myself comparing her features with Parkin's and wondered if he would see a resemblance.

When dinner was over, a servant took Jasmine away to show her a natural hot spring. It gave Parkin and me a chance to be alone. He took my hand and led me out to a secluded garden. His touch warmed my heart. We sat down on a bench facing each other.

"Shriya, I have been thinking of your predicament. You are welcome to stay here for as long as you like. However, as I've told you, the villagers will not welcome you as a single woman with child. You must marry in order to stay here."

"I will not again marry someone I do not love. Do not request this of me, please," I pleaded.

"Shriya, I'm sorry you feel that way. I've always been in love with you. I was hoping you would consider being my wife."

I was dumbfounded. The words echoed in my mind, "I was hoping you would consider being my wife." His wife? The very thing I had dreamed about for years was now possible, and I couldn't think of anything to say.

"Shriya, I love you and asked you to marry me. Was I mistaken to think you would say 'Yes'?"

My eyes dimmed with happy tears. "I've dreamed of being with you for years," I said, as I finally found my voice. "It is hard for me to believe my dreams are actually coming true."

He reached over and embraced me. We held one another close. When at last he released me and looked deep into my eyes, I felt he was looking into my soul. He repeated, "I love you. Will you honor me by becoming my wife?"

"I love you, too, I always have. Yes, I will be honored to be your wife." Excitement vied with relief and filled my soul.

Parkin straightened up. "We must make things right," he declared. "We will need to go back to your town and let your sister know you are safe. Then we can return back here and proceed with the marriage ceremony in which you will become the queen of the island."

"I will be honored to be your queen. It is more than I could ever have dreamed of. But I will not go back and tell my sister; she doesn't deserve an explanation. And I don't trust her. She has threatened to take Jasmine away from me."

"Then we will leave Jasmine here while we travel."

"No. I cannot leave her,"

Parkin shrugged. "All three of us can go, or we can leave Jasmine here. The decision is yours."

"Must we go back?"

"It is the only way I can make you my queen. Otherwise, it could be considered kidnapping and your sister could have the Priest arrest me. Then you would be forced to return."

"Does she have to give her permission? Because she will never do that."

"No. Her permission is not needed. But we must register it with the Priest and notify your sister that we have done so."

A sense of relief overwhelmed me, "Alright, all three of us will go," I said.

"Good, we will leave first thing in the morning. Meanwhile, for your ease and pleasure, do join your daughter in the hot springs."

Yes, I thought, my daughter, our daughter. I would soon have to tell him.

CHAPTER TWENTY NINE

WE ARRIVED IN OUR TOWN early afternoon of the following day. The streets were busy with people. No one seemed to pay any attention to us, and I was thankful for that. We went directly to the Priest's building to register our intended marriage. I was ecstatic. My dream of so many lifetimes was coming true. We were finally going to be together.

The Priest was not happy to see us, and even more displeased with our decision to marry. He argued with us. "It is unusual for members of the royal family to marry anyone but an islander. I have no record of this happening before. I have decided it cannot be allowed."

Parkin responded politely, "Dear Priest, please forgive me. But you do not have the authority to impose this on us. When your family warred against the island many years ago, a treaty was enacted. The island's royal family has the right to marry anyone of their choosing, without restriction. We have fulfilled our part of the treaty. You must fulfill yours."

I became nervous. Could the Priest deny my dream? I watched the Priest contemplate what Parkin had said.

"Alright, I will allow it," the Priest conceded.

I sighed in relief. I glanced at the Priest and saw a smile cross his face. It made me uncomfortable. There was something wrong, I could feel it.

I was happy when the registration was complete but dreaded the next step. We had to face Gwenneth. Well, I had to face her. At least Parkin and Jasmine would be there with me. If everything went well, Gwenneth would not want to make a scene in front of her niece. I doubt she cared what Parkin thought of her. She would consider him the enemy who stood in the way of her plans for Jasmine. I wished I didn't have to deal with this, but if it meant I could spend the rest of my life with the love of my life, then it would be worth it.

We walked down the road to our house. The closer we got, the more anxious I became. Before I knew it, I had to stop and sit down in the road, lest I fainted and fell. After a few moments I felt better. Parkin took my arm and helped me up and we continued our trek. As soon as the house was in sight, Jasmine ran ahead. "Wait!" I yelled, but she kept on going.

When Parkin and I entered the house, Gwenneth was hugging Jasmine. My sister looked up and acknowledged our entrance. "Come, I have tea ready." She gestured towards the table. It was set for four. She had known about our arrival.

We all took seats as my sister poured tea. Jasmine finished hers quickly and ran outside to play with the animals. That left me and Parkin to convey our news. Parkin took the burden of explanation on himself. As he talked, Gwenneth listened. It made me more nervous than I already was, since I knew she never took a passive position. When Parkin was through, she looked at him and said, "I see."

I was stunned. I expected a greater reaction from her, but it did not appear there would be trouble. Relaxing a little, I said, "I would like to pack some more of our things."

"Of course," she replied. "But I have one favor to ask. When I looked into the crystal ball and saw you were coming today, I also saw Janna bringing Christina here at sunset. I will need your help, Sister. Christina is now a young woman. She has been poisoned and is near death. I am unable to do the healing by myself. I beg your assistance. We will be fortunate if we are able to save her at all."

"How has she been poisoned?" I asked.

"I don't know. But her life is in jeopardy."

"Of course I will help. I remember her well. She was a dear, sweet girl."

"She still is, even though Devon, her father, is a horrible person. Fortunately she inherited more of her mother's attributes." I was surprised at the anger she showed. Gwenneth didn't usually reveal much emotion.

"What is it, Sister? Why so much anger?" I asked.

"It was the Priest's son, Christina's father, who raped me so many years ago."

I couldn't let her know Aunt Kalini shared this information with me long ago. I had to act surprised, and I knew Parkin would be shaken by this news.

"Why wasn't he imprisoned in the tower?" I asked.

"Because he is the Priest's son. The Priest blamed me for bewitching him with my sensuality."

I reached out and placed my hand on top of hers and said, "I am so sorry for your experience, I truly am."

"Thank you," Gwenneth said as she pulled her hand back and stood up. "I will prepare the healing area, so it will be ready when they arrive."

I glanced over at Parkin who hadn't said a word. He leaned toward me and whispered, "See? Everything will be fine." But it didn't feel fine. Something was wrong but I didn't know what.

I went outside to find Jasmine, so we could talk. I hadn't had a chance to fill her in with my plans. I took her hand as we walked out into the woods.

"How do you like Parkin?" I asked her.

"He's very nice. I like him. He lives in a big, fancy palace. I wish we could live in a palace like that. He has servants. I've only heard about such things."

"Would you really like to live there?" I asked her.

"Of course, who wouldn't?" she replied.

I felt a sense of relief as I said, "Well, I'm glad to hear you say that, because my plan is to marry Parkin. That will mean we will be living there with him."

She stopped short, turned and looked into my eyes to see if I was telling her the truth.

"It's true," I said. "Parkin is a man I've loved for many years."

"How do you know him?" she asked.

"I met him many years ago before you were born. He used to come to town on his family's fishing boat. But our paths had crossed in previous lives. This will be the first lifetime we will be able to live together as husband and wife. We have loved each other through many past lives but have never been able to be together. Something has always stopped that from happening. I have loved him for as long as I can remember."

"Will Aunt Gwenneth come with us?"

"No, your aunt will stay here and tend to the land. Someone must keep the place running. It has been in the family for many generations. Some day it will be given to you and your husband."

"I don't want it," she said.

"You are still young, but there will be a day when you'll want to come and carry on the family tradition of caring for the land and animals surrounding this sacred space."

"No, I never want to come back here. I will marry an islander, so I can live forever in luxury like you."

"We have plenty of time to plan your future. We will talk about the expectations of your genetic line when you are older," I said.

"What do you mean expectations? I am a free person to do what I want. You have always told me how fortunate I was to have my freedom."

"You are only free within the expectations of our family line. That is why I married Lusha. It was expected of me," I replied.

"You married my father because you had to?"

"Come, let us walk in silence and enjoy the scenery. It will be a long time until we will be here again." I didn't want to finish this conversation, not now. I would tell her who her father was when the time was right. That time was not today.

We came back from our walk to find Parkin outside chopping wood for Gwenneth. I stopped and allowed myself to glance at him from afar. My feelings were undeniable; I was in love with this man and had been from the first time I saw him. I had loved him for several lifetimes. Now, we would spend a life together, instead of fruitless yearning.

I should have been filled with joy at the thought, but something dark and ominous hung over me. I experienced a strong desire to write a letter to my daughter to tell her who her father was. I could not explain the feeling, nor could I dismiss it. So I went inside and took out the ink and pen and a piece of paper.

> *My darling daughter,*
>
> *I want you to know how much I love you. I lived a very lonely life until I had you. You have brought me so much joy! You will never know how much you mean to me and how honored I am to be your mother.*
>
> *I have something to tell you about your father that will surprise you. He is a wonderful man, and I have loved him for many lifetimes. You were born out of love, not from a pure blood line, but from the love of two people who desired to be together.*
>
> *Although I was married to Lusha, a most worthy person, he was not your father. You were conceived shortly after his death. You are descended from the island tribesmen, the ancient royal family of the island. Your father, the love of my life, is Parkin.*
>
> *Please forgive me for not being honest with you before now. I did not how to tell you this.*
>
> *I love you with all of my heart,*
>
> *Mama*

When it was finished I breathed a sigh of relief. I had written a letter that would reveal Jasmine's real father to her. I put the letter in the cellar with the other sacred material. I wasn't ready to give it to her that day, but would present it before we left for the island. She needed to know the truth. First, I had to tell Parkin. He must know before Jasmine or anyone else found out.

The sun was low on the horizon when Janna came down the road towards our house, pulling a cart in which Christina was lying. I could see from Janna's struggles she was exhausted.

"Please take care of Christina," she said. "The Priest has summoned me and I must appear or he will become suspicious. I will be back in a few hours to fetch her." She looked upset, but I couldn't be concerned about it now; we had a sick young woman to contend with.

Parkin picked Christina up and took her to our treatment area, laid her on the table and left us to do our work. Gwenneth could see she was close to death, and asked me to take her feet. Gwenneth went to her head, and we went into a trance. We raised our energy level to a place of unconditional love and sent beautiful purple light into her frail body. We held the focus for about an hour, yet her body was still in trouble. We took a small break and went outside to discuss our strategy. Gwenneth looked at me and said, "It's her soul. Her soul is not sure she wants to continue on this plane. We can't heal her body, unless, on a soul level, she accepts it."

"I felt some resistance from her, too; but didn't understand what it was," I said. "Why would she not want to stay on this plane? She has her whole life ahead of her."

"There must be some sort of turmoil going on in her life she is having trouble dealing with. I suspect she has been sexually molested," Gwenneth said sadly.

"Who would do such a thing?" I asked.

Gwenneth looked at me impassively and said, "I'm not sure, but it may be her father."

I was sick to my stomach. The thought of such a violent, disgusting act made me ill.

"I do not know for sure," Gwenneth said. "The thought came to me while I was holding her head. Then I started to see some images."

"What images?"

"They're too disturbing to repeat," she said softly.

"What should we do?"

"Let's go in and start again. We need to do everything we can to heal her, so if the soul decides to stay, her body will be ready."

I followed my sister back into the house, and we went back to the work of saving this young woman's life. We worked until we were both too tired to go on. We didn't have the energy to eat the dinner Jasmine fixed for us, let alone look into the future. We let Christina sleep on the treatment table while we both took a spot on the floor where we fell fast asleep. Our rest was abruptly ended by a loud crash at the front door.

Terror shook me as I heard people rush through our small home. I heard Parkin shout, "What is this? What's happening? Let me go, I am the royal king of the tribesmen, you have no authority to touch me!"

A man scooped Christina up in his arms. She screamed as he ran out the door with her. "Stop!" I yelled, "She's sick!"

As I tried to get up, another man pushed me back down. Gwenneth jumped up and was coming at him when he grabbed her arm, swung her around and threw her against the wall, slamming her head against an upright beam. I screamed as her body slumped to the floor, unconscious.

The man turned to me, withdrew his sword and held it at my breast. I looked into his eyes and saw hatred such as I had never seen before.

"You are under arrest for witchcraft," he announced. "The Priest will not allow your evil to continue."

"How is healing his granddaughter evil?" I asked defiantly.

"Woman, shut your mouth!" he yelled.

I could hear Parkin scream my name, then nothing. He had been silenced. Killed? Then I realized I hadn't heard Jasmine.

"Jasmine!" I screamed as loud as I could. I felt a large blow to the side of my head. Blackness filled my mind as I slipped into unconsciousness.

Chapter Thirty

I woke up on a hard floor. My sight was blurry, my head heavy and throbbing with pain. I didn't know where I was. As my sight cleared, I saw my sister lying in a heap on the floor in front of our fireplace. Was she alive?

"Gwenneth?" I whispered, "Gwenneth?"

I heard a noise outside. The men were still here. They came in, picked up Gwenneth, and took her outside. Next they came back for me. A man lifted me off the floor, and threw me over his shoulder like a sack of flour. I felt a thunderous roar as the blood rushed to my head. A few moments later I was placed on the back of a horse behind the rider. I wrapped my arms around his waist to keep myself from falling off. I was still very dizzy. I glanced over and saw Gwenneth lying on her stomach over the back of another horse. We hadn't left yet. Some of the men had torches in their hands. They were going to set the house on fire! I feared the sacred books would be burned forever, and also my letter to Jasmine. The men laughed as they stood outside and watched the flames in the house get higher and higher. The thatched roof went next. The house looked like a giant, fiery blossom. My eyes were filled with its fury, my skin burning with the heat. I lost consciousness again.

When I came too, I realized I was chained up in a corner of a room. I peered through the feeble light and saw Gwenneth lying flat on her back in the opposite corner, also chained. I called to her but she did not respond. In agony and grief I cried a river of tears. I saw images of my previous life in which I fell in love with Parkin, lost him overboard, and as a widow was cast out with an ancient curse. No man would go near me. I lived a lonely life. As those ancient images flooded my mind, I let the tears come and soon felt a sense of relief as a heaviness lifted from me.

Gwenneth stirred. "Sister," I said in a low voice. She moaned as she turned over to her side.

"Sister," I said again. She didn't respond. Then she slowly turned and looked at me, "Shriya?"

"Sister, are you alright?"

She reached up and put her hand on the back of her head. "Yes, I think so. Where are we?"

"I don't know," I answered.

She looked around the room. "We are in a cell. This is the tower. They have imprisoned us again."

Then I remembered the guard said we were under arrest for witchcraft. "Gwenneth, they have arrested us for witchcraft. We have been accused of healing the Priest's granddaughter. Does that mean she lived?"

"I believe so."

"And we are being punished for saving her life?"

"Yes. Those who practice the healing arts are said to be in league with the Gatekeeper. You know that, Shriya. We both have always known the risk we took when we did a healing."

"But it makes no sense to be condemned for saving Christina's life. She is the Priest's granddaughter. If anything, he should be thanking us for preparing her body, so her soul could stay."

"He will not see it that way. It frightens him to know we have powers he does not. In order to justify his position, he must put us in the wrong. If we are children of God and have these powers, what does that say about him?"

"It says he also is a child of God, but misguided. He has not owned his own divinity nor has he recognized the divinity in others."

"To be sure. But if he admits the divinity in everyone he loses power over others. Therefore, he strives mightily to keep the townspeople as worshippers."

She was right. There was nothing more I could say on the subject. "What do you think will happen to us?" I asked.

"They are going to burn us."

"Jasmine, what about Jasmine? What have they done with her?"

Gwenneth closed her eyes, concentrating…hoping to have the answer revealed to her. When she opened them again she said, "I see she is safe and in hiding. Janna has her hidden. However, Parkin is not safe. I saw a vision of him in another cell on the other side of the tower. They intend to kill him, too."

Much as I loved Parkin, Jasmine was uppermost in my thoughts. "Thank God, she is alright," I said.

"Yes," Gwenneth continued. "The sacred work will continue as long as she is alive."

I was guilt ridden. My sister still believed my daughter was Lusha's child.

Gwenneth had compassion in her voice as she said, "She is your child, too. It is sufficient for the work to progress through her."

I looked up in bewilderment, wondering if she knew.

"Yes, I know, and have known for some time. Not at first, I only saw what I wanted to see. But eventually the truth made itself known."

"And you know…..what?"

"Parkin is Jasmine's father."

For Gwenneth to have had that information and guarded my secret for years, was astonishing. I felt a rush of love for her. I had often blamed her unfairly. Now I realized her love for me was greater than her own needs.

"You never said anything."

"It is your story to tell, Sister, not mine. I was so consumed with honoring my soul agreement I forgot to consider that you have free will. Jasmine also. We all have free will and do our best to honor our soul agreements, especially those of us who practice the sacred work. It is imperative to continue the genetic line, so we have a family line to reincarnate into. If the work stops, who would we incarnate into? What family line would we be a match for? Can you imagine having to come into a family of worshippers with our knowledge? Each incarnation should be an evolution of the last. I became so consumed with this idea, I forgot there are many possibilities for the work to continue. I could only see mine. Please forgive me."

I tried to reach over and touch her, but was stopped short by the chains that bound us. "I love you, Gwenneth, and appreciate everything you have done for me," I said. She thanked me and lapsed into silence. It was a kind of farewell. The inevitable could no longer be ignored. We were going to be burned. We had crossed the line; we had saved a life. And that would never be tolerated by the Priest.

The next morning, guards came to retrieve us. We were taken out of our cell and brought to the front of the tower, where a motley crowd had already gathered. I saw Parkin with his hands and legs bound, standing on a raised platform, about to be hanged. They placed a noose around his neck and shoved him roughly toward an opening in the floor of the platform. I screamed in terror as I watched his body twitch and kick, then dangle lifelessly from the rope that held him. The man of my dreams was dead once again.

My sister and I were brought to the stake and tied with our hands behind our backs. Our shoulders touched. A guard torched the pyre of wood piled around us. I could feel the flames rise up around my ankles; I closed my eyes and prayed as I shook with fear, "My beloved God, raise the vibration in my body so I do not feel this pain, allow my spirit to soar quickly towards you. Relieve me from the burden of this physical body."

As I stood there, silently praying to my God, I felt Gwenneth's hand grab mine and gently squeeze it. I felt her love flow through my body. It eased my fear enough to open my eyes. I saw through the smoky haze someone struggling through the crowd. Jasmine! I heard her scream, "They're killing my Mama. They're killing my Mama!"

I closed my eyes again and ask my beloved God to spare her from this scene. My heart ached as I realized how this would affect her; the emotional pain and heartache she would suffer because her mother was accused of healing the sick. The Priest will punish her no matter what she does or does not do, he will hate her just for being my daughter. The daughter of a witch is a stigma she will never live down.

I opened my eyes again and looked over at the Priest as his face broke into an evil smile. His biggest fear is that the townspeople will recognize the divine power which lives within each of them. My sister and I had always been an enormous threat to his control over the people.

As I looked out at the crowd gathered to watch us burn, I saw many of the women and children we had healed over the years. They stood by and said nothing, causing me deep emotional pain that hurt more than the burning flames at my feet. I had dedicated my life to the healing arts and saved many of their lives. Yet it seems they allowed their fear of the Priest to overrule what they knew to be an atrocity.

Then I heard my daughter scream, "Will you not defend them? They have saved many of your lives, will you not save theirs? Will you not stand up to the Priest? He has no power over you, only the power you have given him! Please help. Please! They are killing my Mama!"

I looked over at the Priest, and called, "You can kill my body, for not believing in your God, but you cannot kill my soul. I shall live again!"

The flames burst upward. Then I saw the same man with the deep, blue sparkling eyes I had spoken with in front of the Inn. He smiled at me as his eyes sent a beam of violet-blue light into my forehead. I felt myself becoming lost in a sense of peace, and profound love as I saw an aura of pink and golden hue surrounding his entire body. He continued to smile at me as I wondered who he really was.

Then I heard my sister's voice calling me towards the misty blue sky. I closed my eyes and allowed my mind to focus on creating an energy vortex getting stronger and moving faster within me. I let my spirit soar within it and slowly lifted out of my physical existence. It was a great relief. I had forgotten how heavy a physical body could be. I was now in spirit form, and the relief I felt cannot be described.

I saw the gathered crowd at the tower watch in fascination as the flames consumed our physical bodies. I saw the women and children that my sister and I had healed stand by and say nothing. They stared in fear as they watched the flames slowly engulf our bodies. I watched my daughter collapse in grief. I sent her love and prayed to God to watch over her.

I saw, too, my sister's etheric spirit form. She smiled and held her hand out to me. "Come," I heard her say. "We have another adventure to experience."

ABOUT THE AUTHOR

T ERI HOSKINS LIVES IN THE Pacific Northwest with her two dogs, Zach and Sadie. She has one grown daughter who is a Reading Administrator for middle school children. Teri has been attending a spiritual school called, "Ramtha's School of Enlightenment" (RSE) since 1987, where she studies quantum physics, neuroscience and ancient wisdom. RSE is a school where the students are provided the opportunity to put the sciences and wisdom into practice so they can experience the remarkable first hand. Although this book is fiction, it was inspired by Ramtha's teachings. For more information on RSE, please visit: Ramtha.com.

CPSIA information can be obtained at www.ICGtesting.com
Printed in the USA
BVOW011758041212

307183BV00001B/25/P